Broadway Bound

by Neil Simon

SAMUEL FRENCH, INC.

45 WEST 25TH STREET   NEW YORK 10010

7623 SUNSET BOULEVARD   HOLLYWOOD 90046

LONDON   *TORONTO*

RADIO TAPE AVAILABILITY

Samuel French, Inc. can supply producers with either a cassette or reel-to-reel of the radio tape used in the original production, for a period of 8 weeks, only upon receipt of the following:

1. Name & address of your production organization.
2. Dates & number of performances for your entire run.
3. Deposit of $35.00, which is refunded on safe return to Samuel French, Inc. of the tape in good condition immediately following your production.
4. A rental fee of $10.00 for each performance in amateur situations (NOTE: rental fees for STOCK situations will be $100.00 for each production week.)
5. $6.00 to cover either UPS or first-class postage & handling.

In addition to the above, if used, there is a mandatory *amateur* royalty for the use of the actors' voices, which appear on the tape, of $7.50 per performance. For information for use in STOCK situations, please apply to: Actors' Equity Association, 165 West 46th Street, New York, N.Y. 10036, attention of Equity Stock Business Representative.

Permission for performances of the song "IT HAD TO BE YOU", *in the USA* which appears on the tape, is not included without first obtaining a separate license for said performances from Samuel French, Inc. In addition to other royalties there is a music royalty fee for the use of this song, in connection with *amateur* productions, in the amount of $5.00 per performance with a maximum of $25.00 per production week. STOCK royalty terms quoted upon application.

CANADIAN CAUTIONARY NOTICE

Permission for performances of the song "IT HAD TO BE YOU" are not included. A separate music performance license for the use of this song IN CANADA must be obtained from the publisher: Warner/Chappell Music, Inc., 9000 Sunset Boulevard, Los Angeles, California 90069 - Attention Al Kohn. Please note that written proof of the license from Warner/Chappell is absolutely necessary and must be shown to Samuel French (Canada) Ltd. before the tape will be released. No exceptions made!

DEDICATION

To my mother, my father and my brother

BROADWAY BOUND by Neil Simon was first presented by Emanuel Azenberg at The Broadhurst Theatre, New York City, on December 4, 1986, with the following cast:

KATE	Linda Lavin
BEN	John Randolph
EUGENE	Jonathan Silverman
STAN	Jason Alexander
BLANCHE	Phyllis Newman
JACK	Philip Sterling

RADIO VOICES

ANNOUNCER	Ed Herlihy
CHUBBY WATERS	MacIntyre Dixon
MRS. PITKIN	Marilyn Cooper

BROADWAY BOUND was directed by Gene Saks. The setting was by David Mitchell, the lighting by Tharon Musser, the costumes by Joseph G. Aulisi, the sound by Tom Morse, and Peter Lawrence was the production stage manager.

Broadway Bound

ACT ONE

The year is 1949. We are in the Jerome House in Brighton Beach, Brooklyn, New York—a working class neighborhood about two blocks from the ocean.

It is a two-story frame house. On the first floor we see a living room and dining room separated only by furniture. Stage right is the front door. Outside is a brick stoop and the surrounding houses. Just inside the door is a staircase that leads to the four upstairs bedrooms. In the living room area are a sofa, an armchair and a console radio separating the two. Near the front door is a telephone.

In the dining room area is an old, beautiful dining table and five chairs. Just upstage of the table is a breakfront. The furniture, curtains, wallpaper and carpeting reflect the small portion of Post-war prosperity which has come to the Jerome family.

Upstage center is a swinging door which leads to the kitchen. Stage left and running up the downstage is a windowed porch. The kitchen is accessible either through the center door or from the dining room through the porch. A door from the porch leads to the back yard.

The second floor bedrooms are arranged as follows: JACK and KATE's room is stage right, and BEN's room is stage left. Both are visible only when their doors are open. Fully visible and overhanging the living room are EUGENE and STANLEY's rooms.

5

Both rooms contain a single bed and a desk and chair. EUGENE's room is filled with books. All four bedrooms and the bathroom are connected by a central hallway.

It is about six p.m. on a cold day in February. Snow covers the streets. It is already dark.

KATE JEROME, about 50 and graying, is wearing a sweater to ward off the chill that permeates the house. She is setting five places for dinner. As KATE goes into the kitchen for more dishes, BEN EPSTEIN, KATE's father, about seventy-five, comes out of his bedroom and starts slowly down the staris. He is wearing a heavy cardigan sweater and carrying a brown paper bag. He is wearing his house slippers over his socks. KATE comes out of the kitchen as BEN reaches the closet. She speaks louder to BEN than to anyone else.

KATE. I didn't call you, Pop. It's not time for dinner yet.

BEN. Is it dinner yet?

KATE. (*setting out the flatware*) In about a half hour. No one's home yet. Why don't you stay in your room? It's warmer in there.

BEN. (*taking his coat from the closet*) Maybe I'll walk down to the store and get a cigar.

KATE. There's ice on the street, it's twelve degrees out. Eugene will get you a cigar when he gets home.

BEN. I like cold weather.

KATE. You're always complaining you're freezing.

BEN. I don't like it cold in the house. I like it outside. (*putting on his hat*) I have nothing to read. Maybe I'll go to the library.

KATE. (*coming to BEN*) It's six o'clock. The library is closed. Eugene has a million books upstairs.

BEN. I don't read what he reads.

KATE. He has everything.

BEN. He doesn't have a book about Trotsky.

KATE. You just finished a book about Trotsky.

BEN. One book doesn't cover Trotsky. Thursdays they stay open till seven.

KATE. This is Friday.

BEN. I'll take a chance. (*He starts toward the front door.*)

KATE. You want to fall and slip and break your hip again? You don't even have shoes on. You were going to walk in the snow in your slippers?

BEN. (*returning to the closet*) I'll put on my galoshes.

KATE. What's in the brown paper bag?

BEN. (*sitting on the sofa to put on his galoshes*) Where?

KATE. In your hand. What have you got there?

BEN. Nothing. It's garbage. I was going to throw it away.

KATE. Give it to me. I'll put it in the trash can.

BEN. Will you stop treating me like a child. I'm your father, I'll do what I want. When I'm dead, you can treat me like a child.

KATE. You're not going to the library. You were going someplace else. Where were you going?

BEN. I'll go where I want! (*She grabs his galoshes and throws them into the closet.*) If you don't like it, I'll move in with Blanche. Blanche treats me with respect. Don't interfere with me. (*BEN goes to the closet. KATE stops him at C.*)

KATE. You never go out at six o'clock. Something is going on here. If there's something in that bag that's important, you tell me and I'll bring it there myself.

BEN. The day I can't take care of my own things, they'll be praying for me at the synagogue. (*KATE grabs the bag from BEN.*) Katy, don't!!

KATE. (*looking into the bag*) What is this? Is this your bed sheet? . . . Where were you taking it?

BEN. To the Chinese laundry. They never close . . . I want it back, please.

KATE. You *soiled* your sheet and you didn't want to tell me? Why? I've been washing your bed sheets since I'm ten years old . . . So you had an accident. It's alright, Poppa.

BEN. At night I've had accidents. This is the first time during the day.

KATE. So? What else have I got to do with my time? There's no one in this house anymore any-way . . . Take your coat off. You'll catch cold. (*She goes into the kitchen, taking the bag.*)

BEN. (*calling after her*) Not a word, you promise me? I couldn't stay here if the boys knew.

KATE. (*from the kitchen*) The boys? Who sees the boys? I forgot what they look like.

(*BEN sits on the sofa, still in his hat and coat. He puts his slippers back on and takes a newspaper from his coat pocket and reads. EUGENE MORRIS JEROME comes running down the street, wearing a zip-up jacket with the collar up, and a scarf. He is 23 years old. He bursts through the front door and blows on his hands. The front door is not locked. Don't forget, this is still only 1949.*)

EUGENE. Oh, my God! Hi, Grandpa! Did you hear? This is the coldest day in the history of the earth. Is Stanley home yet? (*crossing to the closet and yelling upstairs*) STAN???

BEN. What are you yelling for? I hear you.

EUGENE. (*hanging up his coat*) I was yelling upstairs for Stanley . . . Why are you sitting in your coat?

BEN. What?

EUGENE. Why are you sitting in your coat?

BEN. I was going out. Your mother changed my mind.

EUGENE. (*going to the dining table for an apple*) You're better off. It's freezing. I saw a man kissing his wife on the corner and they got stuck to each other. Mr. Jacobs, the tailor, is blowing hot steam on them.

BEN. (*looks at him, concerned*) Two people got stuck?

EUGENE. If they can't get them apart, they're going to have to sew all their clothes together.

BEN. They can't get them apart?

EUGENE. (*straddling a dining chair and facing BEN*) It was a joke, Grandpa.

BEN. That was a joke? (*He rises and starts toward the closet.*) What kind of joke?

EUGENE. I made it up. It's not really a joke. It's just funny.

BEN. To who?

EUGENE. To me.

BEN. So if it's funny to you, what are you telling it to *me* for? (*BEN goes to the closet and hangs up his coat, but leaves his hat on.*)

EUGENE. (*to audience*) The strange thing about my grandfather is, he has totally no sense of humor. None. But everything he says I think is funny. Maybe because he doesn't mean it to be. If he tried to be funny, he wouldn't be. (*to BEN*) Where's Mom?

BEN. What kind of animal wears a zipper?

EUGENE. A zipper? I don't know. What kind?

BEN. A horse fly.

EUGENE. (*to audience*) See what I mean?

BEN. (*crossing back to the sofa*) *That's* a joke! Not two people got stuck together. You understand?

EUGENE. Yes, Grandpa. Thanks for the priceless information. (*to audience*) My mother and father are the same way. I could say something so funny that the pictures on the wall would get cramps from laughing, but those three just stare at me like dead bodies. I'm trying to become a comedy writer some day and this is the encouragement I get.

BEN. What kind of fish sings an opera?

EUGENE. What kind of fish sings an opera? . . . I give up. What kind?

BEN. A halibut.

EUGENE. A halibut?

BEN. I got it wrong. I thought it was a halibut, but it doesn't sound right.

EUGENE. (*to audience*) Okay? I guarantee you that a halibut is funnier than the real answer . . . I mean, look at him. Sitting there with a hat on. If he put it on to be funny, it would be dumb. But he doesn't know he's got it on, so its hysterical.

BEN. Does a mackerel sound right?

EUGENE. Don't work on it, Grandpa. It'll come to you. (*to audience*) My brother, Stanley, is the only one who appreciates my humor. When I make Stanley laugh, I feel like Charles Lindbergh landing in Paris . . . And Stanley comes up with great ideas. That's why the two of us teamed up. We're going to be a comedy writing team . . . (*like a radio announcer*) "The Jack Benny Show was brought to you by Lucky Strike and was written by Sam Perrin, Nate Monnister, Milt Josephsberg and Stanley and Eugene M. Jerome." (*He hums "Love in Bloom"* as KATE comes in from the kitchen with dinner plates.*)

---

*Note: permission to produce *Broadway Bound* does *not* include permission to use this song in production.

KATE. (*circling the table, setting plates*) What are you eating an apple for? I made chocolate pudding.

EUGENE. It's not a fatal combination, Mom. Where's Pop? I have to talk to everybody.

KATE. I don't think he'll be home for dinner.

EUGENE. Again? That's twice this week. So what are you setting his place for?

KATE. The hell with him, that's what I'm setting his place for. (*She returns to the kitchen.*)

EUGENE. (*crossing to sit beside BEN on the sofa*) Grandpa? What's wrong with Mom? Did she and Pop have another fight?

BEN. It's none of my business.

EUGENE. You know what's going on. She talks to you. You can tell me.

BEN. She *used* to talk to me. She doesn't talk to me anymore.

EUGENE. She snaps at everybody now. Even Stanley can't get a rise from her . . .

BEN. She was always like that. As a child, she could shut off for a month.

EUGENE. I can't picture her as a girl. Was she really supposed to be such a good dancer?

BEN. I only saw her dance once. I didn't like to go to those places. She used to win cups at the er . . . the er . . . that dance place.

EUGENE. The Primrose Ballroom?

BEN. At the er . . . that place near Long Beach.

EUGENE. The Primrose?

BEN. It was a big dance place in those days . . . The Primrose Ballroom!

EUGENE. Right. (*to audience*) Even his timing was terrific . . . He was the greatest teacher of comedy I ever met . . . Only he didn't even know I was studying him.

BEN. Sure, she was a terrific dancer.

EUGENE. She told me once she danced with George Raft.

BEN. Who?

EUGENE. George Raft. The movie actor.

BEN. I know who he is . . . Yeah, sure, she danced with him. He wasn't a star then. He was just a greasy looking kid. He used to go around to all the different ballrooms and pick out the best dancer. She was fifteen, sixteen years old. Not pretty. She was never pretty. But she was graceful on her feet.

EUGENE. Why didn't she ever try to become a professional? Wasn't she good enough?

BEN. (shrugs) She had the accident. She burned half the skin off her back. Twelve girls died in that fire. The owner of that shop went to jail. There was no ventilation, no back door. She couldn't walk for a year . . . She never went down to the beach again. Not with her back like that . . . Her sister, Blanche was a beautiful girl. There were boys lined up outside the house just to look at her. But Blanche couldn't dance a note.

KATE. (entering from kitchen with a pitcher of water and water glasses, which she puts on the sideboard) What are you two talking about?

EUGENE. (crossing to KATE) About when you used to dance with George Raft.

KATE. You see? He still doesn't believe me, Pop.

EUGENE. Who said? I believe you. One day I'm going to write a movie starring George Raft, and he goes into this club, takes your hand and dances a tango with you.

KATE. I did the fox trot better. Make it a fox trot.

BEN. (*crossing to the table*) What was the name of that place where you danced?

KATE. The Primrose Ballroom.

BEN. (*to EUGENE*) That was it. The Primrose!

EUGENE. Okay. Listen, everybody. I have major news. This is serious.

KATE. Where's Stanley? The pot roast is almost dry.

EUGENE. Listen to me, will you? I have to talk to you.

KATE. Pop? You want a little wine tonight?

BEN. No wine for me. Too much acid. I'll have a beer.

KATE. We're out of beer.

BEN. You got wine?

EUGENE. (*to audience*) If I could just get these two on television. (*to KATE*) Will you please come in here and sit down. I have spectacular news for this family.

KATE. (*bringing in relishes from the kitchen*) What family? You see a family in here?

EUGENE. Please sit. (*He seats BEN US. of the table and KATE at the left end of the table.*) Okay . . . Ready? I wish to announce, that your youngest son, Eugene Morris Jerome — is getting married. (*a beat of silence*)

BEN. A Jewish girl?

KATE. He's kidding, Pop. He's not even going with anyone, how's he getting married?

EUGENE. True! True! I am not going with her — yet! But I've seen her. Her name is Josie. I talked to her. I had lunch with her. I saw the color of her eyes. This is marriage, Mom. This is the girl for the rest of my life.

KATE. This is the same girl you met last summer?

EUGENE. No, no! I hate that girl. I never liked her.

KATE. You went with her for a whole summer.

EUGENE. I had nothing else to do. She was nice on the first date . . . *Part* of the first date. Until nine-thirty.

BEN. He liked a girl until nine-thirty?

KATE. He's kidding. That's a joke.

BEN. That's a joke, too? Ask him to tell you about the people who got stuck together.

EUGENE. This girl is serious. I knew it the minute I saw her. Her father owns a music company on the same floor where I work. She writes poetry. She paints. Her father hung her paintings all over his office. She's incredible. She plays tennis. She plays golf. She plays softball. She's been to Europe. She hums *Bach* and Beethoven, and she can whistle Rachmaninoff. She has jet black hair and olive skin, and when she walks down the street, construction workers fall into the cement. If I live to be a hundred, I'll never meet a girl like her again.

KATE. She likes you too?

EUGENE. *Likes* me? I took her to lunch, and we ate from the same chop sticks. We couldn't stop talking. Philosophy, literature, sports . . . Yeah, she likes me alright.

KATE. I never heard you so excited about a girl.

EUGENE. There's one minor complication, though. She's engaged to be married.

BEN. She's what?

KATE. He's kidding. It's another joke.

EUGENE. No. Really. She's engaged to a Harvard Law student. But I'm not worried. I think I have the inside track.

KATE. (*getting up and going into the kitchen*) I have to check the pot roast.

EUGENE. (*calling into the kitchen after KATE*) She's breaking it off. She's not in love with him. She told him, but he doesn't care. He wants to marry her anyway. That's how great she is. (*as KATE comes out of the kitchen with BEN's wine*) If she was marrying him, would she have had lunch with me today?

BEN. Maybe she's looking for wedding gifts.

KATE. (*setting out napkins*) She sounds fickle, if you ask me.

EUGENE. I want to bring her to dinner next week. I want her to meet the family.

KATE. It's been a long time since this family ate together.

EUGENE. On a Sunday. Everybody's home on Sunday. Alright?

KATE. We'll see. Who knows what'll happen by then. I'm sure she's a nice girl, but eat from your own chop sticks. (*KATE returns to the kitchen. EUGENE crosses toward the stairs.*)

EUGENE. (*to BEN*) She never turned down a chance to cook for someone before . . . Something's wrong between her and Pop, isn't there? (*looks back at BEN*) Grandpa? Did you hear me? (*to audience*) He's sleeping. He's probably working on the halibut joke.

KATE. (*coming out of the kitchen and calling up after EUGENE*) Where are you going? We're eating soon.

EUGENE. I'm not leaving the country.

(*EUGENE goes into his bedroom, turns on the light and begins to write in his journal. KATE returns to the kitchen. STANLEY JEROME comes walking briskly down the street. He is 28, wearing a suit, tie, overcoat and hat. He wipes his shoes carefully on the front mat, then enters the house. He is very excited.*)

STAN. (*hanging his coat in the closet*) Grandpa? Is Eugene here? (*screaming upstairs*) GENE!!

BEN. (*waking abruptly*) What the hell are you screaming for?

STAN. I'm sorry. I didn't know you were sleeping.

BEN. Then ask me. If you asked me, I would have told you.

KATE. (*entering from the kitchen*) You walk in the snow without rubbers? The pot roast is half dry. Tell Eugene it's dinner.

STAN. We haven't got time, Mom. We'll take a sandwich later.

KATE. What do you mean? No dinner? (*Upstairs, EUGENE puts down his journal and comes downstaris.*)

STAN. We have to get right to work. (*again, shouting upstairs*) GENE!!

KATE. I've been cooking since two o'clock. Your father doesn't come home. You tell me no dinner. What am I, a slave here? . . . Sit down, Poppa! It's ready!

EUGENE. (*at the foot of the stairs*) What's up?

STAN. (*to EUGENE*) What are you doing now? Whatever you're doing, forget about it. Back upstairs. We've got to start in right away. Mom, no calls for us. Take a message, we'll get back to them. We may be up all through the night, so don't get nervous if you hear us yelling. (*to EUGENE*) Come on! Let's go. We're wasting time. (*STAN starts to dash upstairs.*)

EUGENE. You mind telling me what this is about?

STAN. (*on the stairs*) We got a job at C.B.S.! The Columbia Broadcasting System.

EUGENE. *WHAT???*

STAN. I can't believe how much I did today. I was running all over town. I met everybody. I mean, I would make a terrific agent. I talked to these people like they were my friends . . . I met Abe Burrows! He said to me, "Good luck, kid." . . . (*to an uncomprehending KATE and BEN*) Abe Burrows, the greatest comedy writer in the business . . . I was on the executive floor, long hallway, pictures of every star in the history of C.B.S. — Jack Benny, Ed Sullivan, Arthur Godfrey, Edward R. Murrow.

KATE. You met them?

STAN. No. Their pictures. (*to EUGENE*) There's too much to tell. I haven't got time. We have to start working. I'm so excited, I'm still shaking. Come on, let's go!

EUGENE. (*as STAN again starts up the stairs*) Wait a minute! You mean the regular C.B.S.?

STAN. No, the fake one!

KATE. Can't you talk this over at dinner?

STAN. Is that all you care about? Your dinner? The most important thing that ever happened in our lives, and you're worried about a lousy pot roast?

KATE. (*Obviously hurt, she goes to the kitchen*) Just like your father. You're getting to be just like your father every day. Next thing you'll turn Eugene against me, too.

STAN. I'm sorry! . . . Mom? Ah, shit! (*to EUGENE*) Come on. (*EUGENE and STAN run upstairs, as KATE comes charging out of the kitchen.*)

KATE. What did you say?

BEN. (*ushering her back into the kitchen*) He didn't mean anything. (*EUGENE and STAN go into STAN's room. EUGENE sits in the chair. STAN takes his jacket and tie.*)

EUGENE. Alright, tell me slow. Tell me everything. What kind of a job did we get? When do we start? How much money do we get paid?

STAN. I didn't discuss details. If they like the sketch we bring in, then they'll hire us.

EUGENE. If they like the sketch, then they'll hire us? You mean it's not a job, it's an audition?

STAN. It's a job. They just have to like it first.

EUGENE. I knew it was too good to be true.

STAN. Let me take care of business. I got us the audition, didn't I?

EUGENE. So it *is* an audition. Why can't you say so? I don't mind an audition, but you make it sound like we're leaving for Hollywood tomorrow.

STAN. We discussed Hollywood. I said we would have no problem in moving to Hollywood. We could leave immediately, if they wanted.

EUGENE. C.B.S. asked if we wanted to go to Hollywood?

STAN. No, I brought it up so they would know how we felt. You have to have confidence when you talk to these people . . . That's why I introduced myself to Abe Burrows.

EUGENE. You introduced yourself?

STAN. In the elevator. I said, "Mr. Burrows, the greatest thing that could ever happen to me is to work as a writer on your staff." And he said, "Good luck, kid." And got off on the twelfth floor.

EUGENE. That's why he said, "Good luck"? You made it sound like you had lunch with him or something.

STAN. Did *you* talk to Abe Burrows?

EUGENE. That's not exactly talking to Abe Burrows. That's like the Pope waving to you in the Vatican.

STAN. You say hello to people like that three or four times in the elevator, and after a while they remember you. I'm starving. Do you have anything in your room? Some cookies or something?

EUGENE. Why don't we have dinner first?

STAN. We haven't got time for dinner. We have to work.

EUGENE. If you can eat cookies, you can eat pot roast. It just takes another few minutes to chew it.

STAN. (*pulling EUGENE to his feet*) Alright, go get a couple of sandwiches. We can eat here while we work. And some milk. And some dessert. A piece of cake, whatever we've got.

EUGENE. (*at the door, turning to STAN*) How late are we going to work?

STAN. (*sitting in the chair, pads and pencils ready*) Until we finish. Maybe all night. They want it tomorrow morning at ten o'clock.

EUGENE. They want a finished sketch by ten o'clock in the morning?

STAN. That's how television works. They want it good, but they want it fast. Those shows are on every week, not twice a year.

EUGENE. (*sitting on the ottoman*) We never wrote a sketch in less than three weeks. And we only wrote one sketch . . . And we didn't even finish it . . . And the first part needs rewriting . . . Maybe we're not ready for C.B.S. yet.

STAN. You want me to call them up and tell them that? We'll never hear from them again . . . Once that kind of thing gets around, you're through at *all* the networks.

EUGENE. You mean C.B.S. is going to call N.B.C. and A.B.C. and tell them that two guys auditioning from Brighton Beach can't be depended on?

STAN. Maybe. Do you want to take that chance?

EUGENE. You actually believe that our names are going to come up in a meeting at A.B.C. and N.B.C.? We're not even writers yet. You're the manager of boys clothing at Abraham and Straus. I'm in the stock room of a music company. Our names don't even come up where we work.

STAN. (*standing*) What is it, Eugene? Are you afraid? If you're afraid, tell me. You have to have confidence in this world. If you don't have confidence, I'll *always* be in boys clothing and you'll always be in the stock room.

EUGENE. Why will *you* always be in boys clothing if *I* have no confidence? Your career doesn't depend on my confidence.

STAN. Yes. It does. We're a team. I need you; you need me. You have a great comic mind. I'm the best editor and idea man in the business.

EUGENE. You really believe that?

STAN. Absolutely. I have an eye for talent, and we have talent. When Joe DiMaggio came up from San Francisco, didn't I say he'd become one of the greatest ball players of all time?

EUGENE. Because he was already a great ball player in San Francisco. Why are we so great? We sold three comedy monologues to a guy who plays weddings and Bar Mitzvahs.

STAN. Right. And his salary has tripled in three months. Now all the young comics are starting to come to us. How do you think I got in to C.B.S.? My friend, Mort Garfield, the press agent, showed the monologues to the head of Comedy Development . . . Eugene, I'm going to get us everything we ever dreamed of. If you don't have faith in us, I have enough for both . . . Please trust me . . . Now go get the sandwiches. I want to start working on some ideas.

EUGENE. I didn't know we were going to work tonight.

STAN. Well, we are . . . Put some lettuce on my sandwich. And mayonnaise.

EUGENE. The thing is, I wanted to see this girl tonight.

STAN. Well, now you won't see her. And get me some cucumbers.

EUGENE. I could leave by seven and be back by nine. I could write on the subway. I just have to see her.

STAN. You can see her another night. What's wrong with you?

EUGENE. She's engaged to a guy from Harvard. She wants to break it off, but he's coming in tomorrow to talk her back into it. If I don't convince her I'm the guy for her, he's liable to talk her into going through with it.

STAN. If he can talk her into it, what do you want her for?

EUGENE. Because she's perfect. And you only get one chance in your life of meeting a perfect girl.

STAN. You know how many perfect girls there are in Hollywood? They're *all* perfect. In two years you'll be *sick* of perfect girls. You'll be begging for a plain one. (*EUGENE goes to his own room and begins to dress for his date. STAN is in pursuit.*)

EUGENE. An hour and a half, that's all I'll be gone. If I don't talk to her face to face, I'll lose her, Stan. I know it.

STAN. Eugene, as much confidence as I have in us, I don't have that much confidence that we can write the sketch by tonight. But we have to try. Remember the story Pop told us? How he had the opportunity to go into his own business with a friend . . . how he stayed up all night thinking about it . . . and he couldn't make up his mind. A week later it was too late. His friend lives on Park Avenue now, and Pop is still cutting raincoats . . . Maybe this is the only chance we'll ever get. Maybe not. But are you willing to risk everything for a girl you might not even be interested in by next week?

EUGENE. I'll be interested in her for the rest of my life.

STAN. Then go out with her. Take as much time as you

want. I'll write the sketch myself. (*storming back to his own room*) I mean it. I'm not going to blow this opportunity.

EUGENE. Never mind. I won't see her.

STAN. I said, I'll do it myself.

EUGENE. (*going downstairs*) Don't do me any favors.

(*KATE and BEN enter from the kitchen. KATE puts BEN's soup on the table. He sits down to eat.*)

KATE. (*to EUGENE*) Are you eating or not?

EUGENE. (*going into the kitchen*)We're having sand-wiches upstairs, so N.B.C. and A.B.C. won't be mad at us.

(*KATE follows EUGENE into the kitchen. BLANCHE MORTON, KATE's sister, comes down the street. She wears a mink coat and fur hat. She looks very prosperous. She rings the doorbell. No one answers. BLANCHE opens the door and walks in. She crosses into the dining room. We can sense some tension between BLANCHE and BEN.*)

BLANCHE. Hello, Poppa.

BEN. (*glancing up from his soup*) Who's that? Blanche? I didn't hear the limousine pull up.

BLANCHE. It's not a limousine, Poppa. It's just a plain Cadillac. (*She kisses BEN. He is clearly uncomfortable.*)

BEN. Like John D. Rockefeller is just a plain businessman.

BLANCHE. (*putting her purse and gloves on the sofa*) It got stuck in the snow, just like other cars. I had to walk the last two blocks . . . Where's Kate?

BEN. What happened to the colored fella who drives you around?

BLANCHE. Robert? He's still with us. He was calling a garage to get us pulled out.

BEN. You pay him enough money, he could have carried you here.

KATE. (*entering from kitchen*) Why didn't you tell me you were coming? I could have made extra dinner.

BEN. (*to KATE*) Why? Somebody's eating it besides me?

BLANCHE. Thank you, Kate. I didn't come for dinner. I wanted to talk to Poppa.

KATE. You had to come out in this weather? We have a telephone now, too, you know. (*Everything seems to be an innuendo about the differences in their economic standing. EUGENE enters from the kitchen.*)

EUGENE. (*crossing down to KATE*) Mom, I'm having trouble with the pot roast.

KATE. What did you do?

EUGENE. Hello, Aunt Blanche.

BLANCHE. Hello, Eugene.

EUGENE. I didn't slice it right. I shredded it. It looks like shoe laces.

KATE. I told you to let me do it. What do I bother cooking for? (*KATE goes into the kitchen.*)

EUGENE. (*to BLANCHE*) How's Nora?

BLANCHE. She's fine. Her children are wonderful. She thinks the new baby looks just like you. He's going to be so handsome.

EUGENE. Is that what she said? What did she name him?

BLANCHE. Myron Isaac.

EUGENE. Myron Isaac. (*to audience*) Myron Isaac Eisenberg. Poor kid. Wait till he tries to date a girl from Mount Holyoke.

KATE. (*shouting from kitchen*) EUGENE! WHAT DID YOU DO TO THIS MEAT??

EUGENE. (*going slowly into the kitchen*)I KILLED IT! IT WAS HIM OR ME, MA!! I KILLED THE POT ROAST!!

BLANCHE. (*waiting for EUGENE to disappear into the kitchen, and turning to BEN*) Momma is sick, Pop.

BEN. That's a beautiful coat. What do you need a Cadillac for with a coat like that?

BLANCHE. The doctor tells me if I don't move her to Florida, he can't guarantee what'll happen to her.

BEN. I thought we had a bargain.

BLANCHE. (*sitting on the sofa*) Not talking about Momma is not a bargain, Poppa. It's a punishment. To me, to Momma, to the whole family. And I'm not leaving here tonight until we talk about her.

BEN. (*rising and crossing to BLANCHE*) Who's stopping you? Take her to Florida. She'll outlive the palm trees, believe me.

BLANCHE. You can be so cruel sometimes.

BEN. What did I say? I wished her a long life. You come here and aggravate me while I'm eating my dinner, and *I'm* cruel?

BLANCHE. Do you know what she says to me at night? The very last thing before she goes to bed? She says to me, "Why does that man hate me so much?" What do I answer her, Poppa?

BEN. (*crossing to the armchair*) You don't. Because she'll ask it again tomorrow. Her whole day is built around, "Why do I hate her so much?" She sits on park benches and asks strange women why I hate her so much.

BLANCHE. Why do you?

BEN. Who said I did? *She* did, I never said it . . . I have feelings for the woman, I always will . . . But I can't live her kind of life, she knows that. I hope she lives another fifty years, whether it's on Park Avenue or in alone? A woman who doesn't know a thing in this world except how to serve someone? If she can't make dinner for somebody, her life is over . . . You take your mother to Florida. You take care of her. But as long as I'm alive, I'll eat in this house.

EUGENE. (coming out of the kitchen with a tray of sandwiches) Your dinner will be ready in a second, Grandpa. Mom is sewing the pot roast back together. (*EUGENE starts up the stairs, stopping at the top.*)

BLANCHE. Maybe Jack won't leave. Maybe they'll work things out.

BEN. Maybe . . . I'll stay here until "maybe."

BLANCHE. I would do anything in the world for Kate. But I've got to take care of Momma first . . . If I bring her down to Florida, I can only stay a few weeks. I can't leave Saul to spend the winter in New York alone. She doesn't know anyone down there. She cries now when she thinks about it. Stay with her until Spring . . . Until April . . . Kate is strong. She can take care of herself.

BEN. When did your mother ever have trouble making friends? In two weeks down there she'll be running for Mayor . . . If she gets sick, if she needs me, I'll come to her . . . I have my own work to do. This country is getting richer every day from war profits. And whose pockets does it go into? To those who had the money before the war.

BLANCHE. Poppa, I'm not equipped to argue these things with you. I don't understand them. I never did. But I respect what you think is right. All I'm saying is, does it have to be in Brighton Beach? Can't you change the world from Florida?

BEN. You can change your bathing suits in Florida. Not the world.

BLANCHE. (*crossing to the front door and looking out*)

Why do we have so much trouble understanding each other?

EUGENE. (*entering STAN's room with the tray of sandwiches*) Aunt Blanche is here. She's trying to get Grandpa to . . .

STAN. Shut up! Don't say anything! I'm thinking.

EUGENE. (*sitting in the chair*) Have you got an idea?

STAN. Will you shut up?

EUGENE. Tell me so I can think about it, too.

STAN. It's not an idea yet. It's the beginning of an idea. It's just a thought. A germ. A timy speck in my mind. (*He inspects his sandwich.*) You forgot the cucumbers.

EUGENE. How about a college sketch? College sketches are always funny.

STAN. (*interested; sitting on the ottoman*) Like what?

EUGENE. Like this girl, Kathy O'Hara, from Mount Holyoke goes out on a blind date with a guy named Myron Isaac Eisenberg.

STAN. I hate funny names. It's a cheap way of getting a laugh.

EUGENE. I don't know. Why don't you try it out on Aunt Blanche?

BLANCHE. What if, God forbid, Jack *did* leave her? What if the boys moved out? Saul and I can take care of her. She doesn't have to stay here. We could get a place in Florida for all three of you. Then you wouldn't have to worry about Kate *or* Momma. (*EUGENE leaves STAN's room and returns to his own.*)

BEN. (*rising and returning to his place at the dining table*) You think she would leave this house? You think she would take charity from her own sister?

BLANCHE. (*crossing above the sofa*) I took it from her when I needed it. Where was I going to go when Dave died? There's no shame in it when it's your own family. I would be paying her back for what she did for me and the girls.

BEN. Don't you know your own sister better by now? . . . No. I don't think you do.

BLANCHE. (*crossing below the sofa*) Sometimes, Poppa, I think you don't approve of me . . . Sometimes, I think you don't even like me very much.

BEN. I have three daughters, and I love them the same. But the one who's in trouble is the one that I help.

BLANCHE. Doesn't that include your own wife? Why am I the only one in the family who wants to help Momma?

BEN. Because you're the only one who can afford it. Don't ask for too much, Blanche. When you live on Park Avenue, sympathy doesn't come with it. (*BLANCHE sits on the sofa.*)

EUGENE. (*coming back into STAN's room*) What's new inside the old brain, Stan?

STAN. You're still an infant. I have a God damn infant for a partner. Why don't you wait in your room. I'll call you when I think of it.

EUGENE. I want to help you.

STAN. I said, "Come back when I call you."

EUGENE. (*At STAN's door*) Yes, Heathcliffe. I'll be waiting on the moors. (*EUGENE returns, again, to his own room and sits at the desk.*)

STAN. And bring up the cucumbers!

EUGENE. (*to audience*) It's very hard writing with your brother because your whole relationship gets in the way. Can you imagine *Hamlet* written by William and Harvey Shakespeare?

(*KATE comes out of the kitchen with a hot plate of pot roast and vegetables, which she puts in front of BEN.*

*She also has a small box wrapped in gift paper, which
she gives to BLANCHE.)*

KATE. This is for Nora's baby. If Nora doesn't like the
color, I can exchange it.

BLANCHE. I'm sure she'll love it. She's coming over
Sunday with the baby. (*more to BEN than to KATE*) It
would be a wonderful time for the whole family to get
together. Before Momma leaves for Florida . . . Please
come.

KATE. It's a long trip on the train for Poppa.

BLANCHE. I could send a car.

BEN. A socialist sitting in the back of a Cadillac with a
colored man driving?

BLANCHE. You can let me know at the last
minute . . .

KATE. You sure you can't stay for dinner?

BLANCHE. I told her we'd start to pack tonight. If I
don't help her, she'd try to get her furniture in the suitcase . . . Poppa? Would you *call* Momma during the
week and just say hello?

BEN. I have a lot of meetings this week.

KATE. He'll call.

BEN. If I find the time.

KATE. He'll call.

BLANCHE. (*crossing back to KATE*) I wish I could
stay. I wish we had more time to talk. I'll call you tomorrow. (*She collects her things.*) Sometimes I miss this
house so much. I miss how good we were to each other.
(*BLANCHE kisses KATE on the cheek.*)

KATE. Blanche! I need to talk to you. Not on the
phone. Can we meet someplace in the city? Let me take
you to lunch. Tomorrow, the next day. Whenever you
can find time.

BLANCHE. Of course, Kate. Tomorrow. As early as you want.

KATE. (*tears welling in her eyes*) I hate to ask you this. You know I never like to be obligated to anyone. But you're the only one I . . . (*Suddenly, BEN, who appeared to be nodding off at the table, drops his fork onto the plate. His breathing is heavy.*) Poppa? What's wrong? (*He is holding onto the table to balance himself.*)

BLANCHE. (*dropping her bag and package on the sofa*) Oh, my God!

KATE. (*taking BEN's hat off*) What is it, Poppa? Is it a pain? Is it your chest?

BLANCHE. (*rushing to BEN*) Oh Poppa!

KATE. Try to breathe slowly. Deep breaths, Poppa.

BEN. (*sitting up straighter*) It's alright. I'm alright.

KATE. You want some water? (*Pours him a glass of water*) Drink some water.

BLANCHE. (*taking BEN's hand*) His hands are cold as ice.

KATE. Do you want to lie down?

BEN. I got dizzy for a second. (*now fully recovered; To KATE:*) I was hungry. You could wait forever for something to eat around here.

BLANCHE. It's this climate. Two blocks from the ocean in February, how can you keep the cold out of the house?

BEN. It's not the cold. It's not the climate. It's nerves, that's what it is.

KATE. How do you know it's not your heart? You haven't seen a doctor in over a year.

BEN. A heart attack God gives you. Nerves you get from people who worry about you too much.

BLANCHE. Is that meant for me, Poppa?

KATE. It was meant for both of us. You learn not to pay attention. He doesn't mean it.

BLANCHE. He can't stand the winters here any more than Momma. (*She sits at the table.*) I don't mean to upset you, Poppa. If you're happier here, then stay. Forget what we talked about. I'll get somebody to stay with Momma. I'll work it out myself.

KATE. (*returning BEN's hat to the closet*) Alright, Blanche. Leave it alone for now. We've got time yet.

BLANCHE. (*to BEN*) Why is it so hard for us to talk to each other? Why is it so hard for you to take anything from me? I'm afraid to kiss you when I see you, I know how uncomfortable it makes you . . . Why is that, Poppa?

BEN. (*banging his fist on the table*) YOU ASK TOO MUCH OF ME! (*KATE and BLANCHE are stunned by this outburst.*) I am not an affectionate man. I don't trust affection . . . Sometimes people give it to you instead of the truth.

BLANCHE. (*visibly hurt, going to sofa to collect her purse and package*) I see . . . And what's the truth about me, Poppa? Have I betrayed you because the man I married became wealthy? When I met him, he was on the verge of bankruptcy. Whatever he got, he earned. Whatever he has, he worked for.

KATE. Blanche, stop it. That's enough. Everybody has said enough.

BEN. Let her say what she wants. She's a good girl, my Blanche, but sometimes she forgets where she came from . . . Is it cold outside, Blanche? You bet your life it is . . . Is it hard on the people who live out here? Ask them, they'll tell you . . . Take them *all* to Florida, they'll put up a statue of you on the boardwalk . . . But not even Saul could afford that. They all can't escape, Blanche. They all don't get a ticket to Miami.

BLANCHE. And my sin is that I can afford to buy you one?

BEN. There's no sin, Blanche. You're a generous woman. Even *I* can see that. I thank God you're able to take care of your mother. But I can't enjoy the benefits of a society that made my daughter rich and starves half the people in the country.

BLANCHE. I can't take care of all the people in the country. I didn't ask for all this. I was happier when I had no money and Dave was alive. But I'm not going to curse God because He gave me a kind and loving husband and yes, a mink coat and a Cadillac car. You want them, take them. I didn't ask for it. I found the coat in my closet on my birthday. Some good it does me. It keeps out the cold, but it also stops my father from reaching out and holding me . . . Is that the politics you believe in, Poppa?

BEN. I believe in what I was taught from the day I was born.

BLANCHE. I believe in what I was taught, too . . . I was taught that a family who loves each other takes care of each other . . . You're seventy-seven years old, Poppa, you've done enough. You've worked hard all your life. It's time to play pinochle and walk on the beach. Maybe you'll meet a few retired Socialists. (*going to KATE*) I'll see you tomorrow, Kate?

KATE. Let me see what happens. I'll call you in the morning.

BLANCHE. (*walks to the door, then turns to look at BEN*) I love you, Poppa . . . and I'll accept whatever affection you can give me. But you're not going to stop me and Momma from giving you ours. We're women, we don't know any better. (*BLANCHE exits.*)

EUGENE. (*from his bedroom, to audience*) Can you see now why I want to write comedy? Even God has a terrific sense of humor. Why else would He make Grandpa a dedicated Socialist, fighting against the wealthy class, and then give him a daughter who marries the richest guy in the garment district? I wonder if we could sell it to C.B.S.? (*KATE clears away EUGENE's, STAN's and her place settings. Then she turns out the porch light.*)

KATE. Why don't you finish your dinner?

BEN. I'm not hungry anymore.

KATE. You'll change your mind. I'll leave it in the oven. (*KATE takes BEN's plate and starts toward the kitchen.*)

BEN. You think I don't know what's going on between you and Jack? That's what you wanted to talk to Blanche about, wasn't it?

KATE. You spoke to Jack?

BEN. I spoke to nobody. But you don't get to be seventy-seven without noticing a few things.

KATE. Nothing's going on.

BEN. If you can tell your sister, why can't you tell me?

KATE. I don't know. Maybe I'm afraid you'll think it's all my fault.

BEN. Is it?

KATE. You see? That's why I'm afraid to talk to you.

(*KATE exits into the kitchen. BEN goes upstairs to his bedroom. EUGENE speaks from his bedroom to the audience.*)

EUGENE. There's so much material in this house. Maybe I don't have to become a writer. If only I could get enough people to pay for seats in the living room.

STAN. (*bursting into EUGENE's room, holding a sheet of paper*) I can't believe it. I cannot believe it!

EUGENE. What?

STAN. I just came up with an idea. One of the funniest ideas I ever heard of in my life. I was hysterical just picturing it.

EUGENE. So what's wrong?

STAN. I just remembered I saw it on the Red Skelton show three weeks ago. (*He throws the paper into the wastebasket*) Can you imagine if we brought that in to C.B.S.? They would grab us by our collars and crotches and throw us out in front of Abe Burrows.

EUGENE. Well, what was the idea? Maybe we could twist it around.

STAN. Twist it around? We don't make pretzels, we write comedy. We're supposed to be original, think of *new* things. We don't steal from other people's shows.

EUGENE. What are you, the District Attorney of Comedy?

STAN. We're wasting time again. What have you got?

EUGENE. *Me*? I don't have anything.

STAN. Then what were you doing all this time?

EUGENE. I was thinking of a way to grow cucumbers in my bedroom.

STAN. God, you are lazy! Let me ask you something.

EUGENE. Oh, God! I hate it when you say, "Let me ask you something."

STAN. Let me ask you something. Are you serious about writing or not?

EUGENE. Yes.

STAN. Yes, what?

EUGENE. Yes, I am serious about writing.

STAN. No, I don't think you are.

EUGENE. (*jumping to his feet*) Oh, Jesus! . . . I am, Stanley. I am serious about writing. I'm kind of footloose and fancy-free about cucumbers, but I'm serious about writing.

STAN. You can say what you want, I don't believe you are.

EUGENE. I am! I am! (*to the heavens*) Please, Holy

Mother, make my blind brother see that I speak the truth.

STAN. Alright. Tell me how serious you are about writing.

EUGENE. Let me call a doctor, Stanley. I think you're cracking up.

STAN. I want to know. I want to know just how serious you are about writing.

EUGENE. (*spreading his arms out wide, as though measuring a fish*) This much!

STAN. Don't get sarcastic with me.

EUGENE. That wasn't sarcastic. I was telling you point blank I think you're crazy.

STAN. You've been writing your memoirs since you're fourteen years old, and you still don't give a God damn about your craft.

EUGENE. It's not a craft, Stanley. A craft is Indian rug weaving. My memoirs is putting down the nutty things that have happened in my life. And this conversation is getting a whole chapter of its own.

STAN. That's exactly what I mean. You may say you're serious about it, but you don't *act* serious.

EUGENE. You want me to act serious about writing? . . . Okay. Watch! (*He strikes a very grim pose.*) I would rather write a comedy sketch than feed all the starving children in the world. (*He falls to the floor at STAN's feet.*)

STAN. I could kill you right now. You want to forget about this? You want me to call C.B.S. and tell them we're just not ready for this yet? Huh? Huh? Alright?

EUGENE. What are you getting so angry about?

STAN. I'm not angry.

EUGENE. Yes, you are.

STAN. I'm angry about your attitude.

EUGENE. So why did you say you're not angry?

STAN. Your attitude stinks, you know that?

EUGENE. I can't believe this! Maybe to *you* my attitude stinks. To me, my attitude smells wonderful.

STAN. (*going to the door*) Listen, let's just forget about it. I don't think we can work together. I'm getting older, I don't have any more time to waste. I'll find somebody else.

EUGENE. How about Abe Burrows? He's probably waiting for you on the elevator.

STAN. No, that's what I'm going to do. I'm going to find somebody else. Someone with a bigger interest in his career than you have.

EUGENE. (*spreading out his arms again*) You mean bigger than this?

STAN. You've got a lot to learn, my young friend.

EUGENE. "My young friend"?? . . . Jesus, now you're Abraham Lincoln! (*STAN storms out, into his own room. EUGENE follows.*) You know what I think this is all about, Stanley? I think you're scared. I think it's a terrific way to put off sitting down and writing. That's what I think. (*EUGENE returns to his own room.*)

STAN. (*following EUGENE*) Go on! Go visit your girlfriend! I just hope to God she's got money and is willing to support you, because you'll never make a penny in this world on your own, you little shit! (*He slams EUGENE's door, and goes back into his room.*)

EUGENE. (*to audience*) See what I mean about brothers writing together! . . . They're too busy sibling all the time . . . But in a way, Stan was right. I wasn't concentrating because I was afraid I was losing the greatest girl in the world . . . Being in love is a definite career killer. (*The door opens and STAN comes back in.*)

STAN. I got another idea.

EUGENE. (*to audience*) But lucky for me, Stan was real dedicated. (*to STAN*) What's the idea?

STAN. Not an idea for a sketch. But I know what we've been doing wrong.

EUGENE. You do?

STAN. Tell me what you think we've been doing wrong.

EUGENE. What we've been doing wrong?

STAN. (*nods*) What's the essential ingredient in every good sketch we've ever seen?

EUGENE. I don't know. What?

STAN. Don't say "what" so fast. Think about it.

EUGENE. (*thinks*) What's the essential ingredient in every good sketch we've ever seen.

STAN. Right.

EUGENE. I don't know. What?

STAN. You *do* know. We've talked about it. You're just not thinking.

EUGENE. Stan, I don't want to take a high school exam. Tell me so we can write the sketch.

STAN. The ingredient in every good sketch we've ever seen — is conflict! . . . Remember? Remember the night we talked about conflict?

EUGENE. Yes.

STAN. You *do* remember?

EUGENE. Tuesday, September 7th, eight-thirty-five p.m.

STAN. Alright. Now what's the *other* ingredient in every good comedy sketch we've ever seen?

EUGENE. (*sighs in exasperation*)*More* conflict!

STAN. Come on. You know it . . . Think about it . . . Heh? . . . Do you know it?

EUGENE. Yes. It's when one brother wants to kill the other brother.

STAN. YES!!

EUGENE. Yes? That's it?

STAN. It's close. You said it in that sentence. Do you remember what you said in that sentence?

EUGENE. No. It was too long ago.

STAN. One brother wants to kill the other brother. The key word is *wants!* In every comedy, even drama, some-body has to want something and want it bad. He wants money, he wants a girl, he wants to get to Philadelphia. When somebody tries to stop him from getting money or a girl or getting to Philadelphia, that's conflict. Wanting plus conflict equals what?

EUGENE. (*looking heavenward*) Oh, please, God. Don't let me get it wrong. (*to STAN*) A job at C.B.S.

STAN. Right.

EUGENE. How do you know all this?

STAN. I watch all the comedy shows. I make notes. I figure it out. I think scientifically. That's why I'm good at gin rummy. I always remember what the other guy picks up.

EUGENE. So now that you know all this, do you have an idea for a sketch?

STAN. No. Do you?

EUGENE. Yeah. I think so.

STAN. When did you think of it?

EUGENE. While you were doing all that explaining to me.

STAN. Well, tell it to me.

EUGENE. Okay . . . there's a guy and a girl. They're in bed together.

STAN. Who are they?

EUGENE. No one. Just a guy and a girl.

STAN. I know, but what do they do? Is he a cop? An insurance salesman? A doctor? What?

EUGENE. It doesn't matter.

STAN. Details are always better for a character. If he's a cop, maybe there's some police jokes in it.

EUGENE. Okay. He's a cop. Patrolman John J. Mahoney. Fourth Precinct, 27th District of Manhattan on the night shift, ten to six. His partner is Patrolman Vito Manganezi, and he's married with . . .

STAN. Alright, alright. You are some pain in the ass.

EUGENE. So this cop is in bed with a girl . . . Maybe they're married.

STAN. *Maybe* they're married?

EUGENE. THEY'RE MARRIED! They had a wonderful wedding, four hundred guests catered by the Paramount Caterers . . .

STAN. I said alright! . . . Go on.

(*A loud knock on the bedroom door.*)

BEN. (*from outside the door*) Will you shut up in there! (*STAN opens the door.*) I can't sleep! Go into another business!

EUGENE. We're sorry, Grandpa. (*to STAN*) Come on. (*EUGENE and STAN run downstairs. BEN returns to his room.*)

STAN. Go on, go on . . . They're both in bed.

EUGENE. They're both in bed. She has a broken leg.

STAN. I like that.

EUGENE. Thank God. (*They sit on the sofa.*)

STAN. What time of year? . . . Winter, Spring, Summer?

EUGENE. Winter. (*STAN stares at him.*) Twenty-one degrees, winds fifteen miles per hour, barometer falling . . .

STAN. Did I ask you? Go on.

EUGENE. It's two a.m. The window is open. It's freezing in the room. She asks him to get up to close the window. He rushes over in his pajamas, but the window is frozen. So he pushes down with all his might — and slips his disc. He can't move. She can't move. The window is still open, and they're both freezing to death. How do they close the window?

STAN. How?

EUGENE. I don't know. It's only the beginning. I just thought that two people who can't move in a freezing room with the window wide open was a funny idea. Do you like it?

STAN. (*pacing, thinking*) I like some of it.

EUGENE. I only *told* you some of it. That's all there *is* is some of it . . . What part didn't you like?

STAN. The logic. Why doesn't she call the doctor?

EUGENE. (*sitting in the armchair*) I don't know . . . He's not in. He went to a Broadway show.

STAN. At two in the morning?

EUGENE. They stole his car in the parking lot.

STAN. She could call another doctor.

EUGENE. They're at a convention in Cleveland.

STAN. Every single doctor in New York?

EUGENE. She broke her fingers. She can't dial.

STAN. All ten fingers?

EUGENE. It's just a comedy sketch. Does it have to be so logical? We're not drawing the plans for the Suez Canal.

STAN. Yes, we are. It's not funny if it's not believable.

EUGENE. Oh, you mean The Three Stooges are believable? Moe is fifty-five years old and wears bangs and sticks his fingers in his brothers' eyes.

STAN. (*crossing up to EUGENE*) The Three Stooges? Is that the kind of comedy you want to write? That's for morons.

EUGENE. Really? Well, the morons made it to Hollywood, and the geniuses are freezing in Brighton Beach.

STAN. I'm not going to settle for crap. If we're going to be good, we're going to be the best

EUGENE. Well, I can't think of anything else.

STAN. (*pacing*) Let's keep trying.

EUGENE. Their phone is out of order?

STAN. Too easy. Too coincidental.

EUGENE. Too easy? It took me twenty minutes to think of it.

STAN. (*pacing around the sofa*)Don't give up. Let me tell you the idea again. A guy and a girl are in bed together, okay? It's the middle of winter, and the window is open . . .

EUGENE. What if he's *not* a cop? What if he's a doctor? Then we don't have to worry about calling a doctor.

STAN. If he's a doctor, he fixes them both up. There's no sketch.

BEN. (*shouting from his bedroom*)THAT'S FINE WITH ME!

STAN. So, she has a broken leg. He gets up. It's freezing in the room. He rushes over to close the window . . .

EUGENE. (*leaping to his feet*) . . . and he trips on the wire and pulls out the telephone cord.

STAN. . . . and they *can't* call the doctor! You know what we are, Gene? We're God damn geniuses. (*He kisses EUGENE and they both run upstairs to EUGENE's room.*) Now we can begin! Now we can write the sketch! Come on! (*STAN leaps onto the bed, and EUGENE sits at his desk. EUGENE speaks to the audience.*)

EUGENE. So at ten to seven in the evening, we had the idea for the sketch that would launch our careers, and we began to write. By eleven-thirty that night we had filled up three pads and had not written a single usable word.

(*KATE comes out of the kitchen, and turns on the dining room lights. She sits at the table, waiting. STAN sits up and rubs his eyes.*)

STAN. I can't keep my eyes open. You want to take a half-hour break?

EUGENE. How about an hour?

STAN. Thirty minutes. That's all. You have no discipline. Don't let me fall asleep.

(*STAN exits to his own room, turns off the lights in both rooms. Both lie on their own beds. JACK JEROME, fifty-five years old and wearing an overcoat, rubbers and hat, comes down the street and in the front door.*)

JACK. (*surprised to see KATE*) You still up?

KATE. I thought you might be hungry.

JACK. (*going to the closet to take off his coat and hat*) I had dinner at work. They had food sent in. We have to get the spring line out by next Thursday. (*sitting on the sofa to take off his rubbers*) Everybody's working overtime. Jacobsen is sleeping in his office.

KATE. (*collecting his rubbers and taking them to the closet*) Oh, because you said you might be home tonight.

JACK. No, I told you. The whole week. Maybe into Monday or Tuesday. (*standing and starting toward the stairs*) Everyone's exhausted. It's a wonder they're all not sick.

KATE. I have some tea heated up. Sit with me a few minutes.

JACK. Let me take a shower first. I'm all sweated up. I smell from the cutting room.

KATE. In thirty-three years, it's never bothered me before. I'll get the tea. (*KATE exits into the kitchen. JACK takes off his suit coat and crosses to his seat at the head of the dining table.*)

JACK. (*calling into the kitchen*)How are the boys?

KATE. (*from the kitchen*) I haven't seen them all night. They've been upstairs writing. Stanley thinks they might be able to get something in television.

JACK. Television? Ten people in this country have a television. There's no money unless there's volume. He's better off at Abraham and Straus.

KATE. If he gets this job, he wants to quit. Yesterday he looked for an apartment in the city. I think he and Eugene are getting ready to move out. (*KATE comes in from the kitchen with a tea service.*)

JACK. He's going to pay New York rent on a job he doesn't have yet? He's got a good future at A & S, for God's sake. He's got security there. What do either one of them know about show business?

KATE. (*serving JACK his tea*) It's what they want to do.

JACK. What you want to do and making a living are two different things. You don't keep a roof over your head doing what you *want* to do. You do what you *have* to do.

KATE. I'm not saying you're wrong. But if they don't try this now, when will they ever have the chance?

JACK. A chance at what? It's a one in a million shot. Who knows if they have talent? Did you ever see anything they wrote?

KATE. They read me something once. They got upset because I didn't laugh. They didn't tell me it was supposed to be funny.

JACK. If *you* didn't laugh, what chance do they have with the ten people with television sets? . . . It's crazy. It's not for them. I'll talk to Stanley tomorrow.

KATE. (*sitting down with her own tea*) It's not your decision, Jack. They're grown boys. They do what they want now . . . We don't need their money. It's only you, me and Poppa now. And if Blanche can get Poppa to move to Florida, it'll just be the two of us. (*She pauses, looks at JACK.*) It's a different world today. They have more opportunities than we did. You never had a chance to look around. You took the first job that came along . . . Sometimes I forget what you gave up to take care of a family.

JACK. Was I complaining? Did I say I gave up anything? I wasn't that brilliant or educated to give up anything. But I made the most of what I did. Maybe to some people I didn't accomplish anything important, but as a cutter, I'm one of the best. One of the most respected, ask anybody.

KATE. I don't have to ask, Jack. I *know.*

JACK. You think I don't know what's on Stanley's mind? You think I don't know what he's looking for? . . . Actresses! Showgirls! That's what he's looking for. And for *that* he'll give up security and a future.

KATE. Not everybody's looking for showgirls, Jack.

JACK. Is he afraid of hard work? Is he afraid of putting in regular hours? I've done it for a lifetime, it hasn't killed me.

KATE. No, Jack, it hasn't killed you. But the one thing I was always sorry about was that you never did something with your life that you enjoyed more.

JACK. I don't understand you. I've been a cutter for thirty-three years, why do you bring up a thing like that now for?

KATE. (*stacking the empty cups and plates*) Because you seem different to me now. Because for the first time, I see the unhappiness in your face. You look older to me, Jack.

JACK. I look older because I'm older.

KATE. No. That's not what I see. What I see is disappointment in your eyes.

JACK. (*rising and crossing toward the stairs*) I'll take a shower and get a good night's sleep. It'll be gone in the morning.

KATE. I look every morning and it's never gone . . . Maybe it's *me* you're disappointed with.

JACK. (*stopping at the sofa*) What are you talking about?

KATE. (*taking the tea service into the kitchen*) I don't know what I'm talking about. You tell me, Jack.

JACK. (*calling after her, into the kitchen*) Tell you what? You have something on your mind, then say it.

KATE. (*coming out of the kitchen, to the dining table*) If I say what I'm thinking, you're liable to tell me what I don't want to hear.

JACK. Listen, Kate. I've had a long day. I'm tired. Whatever this is about, we'll talk about it in the morning.

KATE. I want to know what you're planning to do.

JACK. Planning to do about what?

KATE. (*folding the tablecloth, carefully*) Whatever's been going on, I want it to stop. I don't want to know who she is or what she's like. And I don't want to hear any lies. I just want tonight to be the end of it, and I'll never talk about it again, as God is my judge.

JACK. You think I'm carrying on with some woman? Where do you get such ideas from?

KATE. Two things a woman doesn't have to be told. When she's pregnant and when her husband stops loving her. Maybe we've had enough years of loving each other. But I will not live out the rest of my life being humiliated.

JACK. Who's been talking to you? What God damn liars tell you such things? Nothing is going on. What's happened to us when we can't believe each other anymore?

KATE. Maybe it's the way you look at me when you say you're telling me the truth.

JACK. (*deliberately*) There is no other woman.

KATE. Why not?

JACK. What?

KATE. Why not? You're a healthy man, you're affectionate, you're as normal as anyone else. We haven't been together as man and wife since God knows when. So, if it's not me and you're swearing it's no one else, I'm asking you, "Why not?"

JACK. Kate, let's not get into this. I beg of you.

KATE. *Don't beg me!!* . . . Don't tell me how trusting we were. We passed all that when our children grew up. Now it's just you and me, Jack, and if I'm not enough for you anymore, then you tell me and get out. Get out, God damn it! I will not be pointed at from windows as I walk down the street.

JACK. There is no other woman.

KATE. I don't care. Stop it anyway.

JACK. Look, I know I've changed. I know I'm different.

KATE. Yes, you are.

JACK. I've stopped feeling for everything. Getting up in the morning, going to bed at night . . . Why do I do it? Maybe it was the war. The war came along and after that, nothing was the same. I hated poverty, but I knew how to deal with it. I don't know my place anymore.

When I was a boy in temple, I looked at the old men and thought, "They're so wise. They must know all the secrets of the world" . . . I'm a middle-aged man and I don't know a damn thing. Wisdom doesn't come with age. It comes with wisdom . . . I'm not wise, and I never will be . . . I don't even lie very well . . . There was a woman. (*KATE stares at him.*) About a year ago. I met her in a restaurant on Seventh Avenue. She worked in a bank, a widow. Not all that attractive, but refined woman, spoke very well, better educated than I was . . . It was a year ago, Kate. It didn't last long. I never thought it would . . . and it's over now. If I've hurt you, and God knows you have every right to be, then I apologize. I'm sorry. But I'll be truthful with you. I didn't tell it to you just now out of a great sense of honesty. I told you because I couldn't carry the weight of all that guilt on my back anymore. (*JACK waits quietly for her reaction.*)

KATE. How old a woman?

JACK. Don't get into that, Kate. If you want to have your anger, throw something at me. But don't ask me questions about her. Let's talk about you and me. Tell me how we can get through this thing, but who and what she is is not important anymore.

KATE. How old a woman?

JACK. God Almighty, you won't be happy until you dig into it, will you? . . . Forty-four, forty-five, I don't know. I never asked her.

KATE. What did you talk about?

JACK. When?

KATE. That first day in the restaurant.

JACK. I don't remember. We just talked.

KATE. It must have been about something. The soup?

The chicken? The fruit cup? How do these things start, Jack? I never heard one before.

JACK. I don't know who you're trying to hurt more, Kate. You or me.

KATE. What did you say in the restaurant, Jack?

JACK. Anything. Everything. We talked about the weather, about politics, about music, our children . . .

KATE. You get forty-five minutes for lunch. Besides eating, that's a lot of ground to cover, wasn't it?

JACK. Yes, it was a lot of ground to cover. Is that the answer you want, Kate?

KATE. Why her? After thirty-three years of marriage, why is she the one you picked?

JACK. Don't For crise-sakes, don't make me say nice things about her. You want me to say she was a tramp? Okay, she was a tramp. I had an affair with a peroxide blonde tramp, Kate. Is that alright?

KATE. I wish to God you did. A tramp I could handle. But that's not your nature, Jack . . . And I want to know why *this* woman was the one.

JACK. This is a mistake, Kate. A mistake we'll both regret, as God is my judge . . . Why this woman? Because she had an interest in life besides working in a bank or taking care of her house. To her, the world was bigger than that. She read books I never heard of, talked about places I never knew existed. When she talked, I just listened. And when *I* talked, I suddenly heard myself say things I never knew I felt. Because she asked questions that I had to answer . . . Learning about yourself can be a very dangerous thing, Kate. Some people, like me, should leave well enough alone . . . The things you were afraid to hear, I won't tell you, because they're true. It lasted less time than you think, but once was enough to hurt, I realize that . . . I never ate in that restaurant again, and I have never once seen her again . . . If either one of us feels better now that I've told you all that, then shame on both of us. (*JACK sits at the table, opposite KATE. She turns away from him.*) If I killed a man on the street, you would probably stand by me. Maybe even understand it. So why is this the greatest sin that can happen to a man and wife?

KATE. Because I'm not strong enough to forgive it.

JACK. I didn't expect you to.

KATE. What *do* you expect?

JACK. I'm not clever enough to answer that.

KATE. This woman — this refined, educated woman — if I left you, would you go to her?

JACK. She wouldn't have me. She's content with her life the way it is.

KATE. If she *would* have you, would you go to her?

JACK. No.

KATE. Why not?

JACK. Because I know where I belong.

KATE. Here? Is this where you belong, Jack? In a house with a woman who hasn't read the right books or travelled any further in the world than the subway could take her? I take care of a house and I raised a family, but I don't know the questions to ask you that will make you feel things you never felt before. No, I don't think this is where you belong anymore, Jack.

JACK. If I felt that, I would have left last year.

KATE. (*rising*) You did leave, Jack. You never moved out, but you left.

JACK. I know we've not been the same together. Not for a long time. And for that, I'm sorry.

KATE. So you stay with me because she won't have you . . . I got some bargain, didn't I, Jack?

JACK. . . . So? What do you want to do?

KATE. What do *I* want to do? Is that how it works? You have an affair, and I get the choice of forgetting about it or living alone for the rest of my life? . . . It's so simple for you, isn't it? I am so angry. I am so hurt by your selfishness. You break what was good between us and leave me to pick up the pieces . . . and *still* you continue to lie to me.

JACK. I told you everything.

KATE. (*sitting in the US. dining chair*) I knew about that woman a year ago. I got a phone call from a friend, I won't even tell you who . . . "What's going on with you and Jack?" she asks me. "Are you two still together? Who's this woman he's having lunch with every day?" she asks me . . . I said, "Did you see them together?" . . . She said, "No, but I heard." . . . I said, "Don't believe what you hear. Believe what you see!" and I hung up on her . . . Did I do good, Jack? Did I defend my husband like a good wife? . . . A year I lived with that, hoping to God it wasn't true and if it was, praying it would go away . . . And God was good to me. No more phone calls, no more stories about Jack and his lunch partner . . . No more wondering why you were coming home late from work even when it wasn't busy season . . . Until this morning. Guess who calls me? . . . Guess who Jack was having lunch with in the same restaurant twice last week? . . . Last year's lies don't hold up this year, Jack . . . This year you have to deal with it. (*JACK looks at her, remains silent a moment.*)

JACK. . . . It's true. I saw her last week. Twice in the same restaurant, once in another restaurant.

KATE. And where else, Jack? Do you always sit or do you lie down once in a while? (*rising*) Twice tonight I went to the phone to see if you were really working, but I was so afraid to hear that you left early, I couldn't dial the number . . . How is it possible I could hate you so much after loving you all my life?

JACK. Would you believe me if I told you it was lunch and nothing else?

KATE. (*crossing to the stairs*) I can't talk about this anymore . . . Sleep down here. Anywhere you want except next to me.

JACK. She's just a friend now, Kate. That's all.

KATE. Is that what you tell her I am? Just a wife? (*She starts up the stairs.*)

JACK. She left her job for six months. I knew what had happened but I couldn't get in touch with her. Her son was killed in an automobile accident . . . So I have lunch with her and talk about anything else except the accident.

KATE. (*coming back down to the foot of the stairs*) If you see her again, you take your things and move out of this house. (*She starts back up the stairs.*)

JACK. I slept with her before and you forgave me. Now I buy the woman lunch and offer her compassion and for this you want to end the marriage.

KATE. (*coming back downstairs, close to JACK*) I didn't expect to get through a lifetime without you touching another woman. But having feelings for her is something I can never forgive.

(*Kate goes upstairs into her bedroom. JACK sits at the table for a moment, then goes into the kitchen. A subway train is heard in the distance. STAN suddenly sits up in bed. He turns on his light and looks at his watch. He rushes into EUGENE's room and turns on EUGENE's light. He shakes EUGENE.*)

STAN. Why didn't you wake me?

EUGENE. (*struggling out of a sound sleep*)What?

STAN. I told you to wake me at twelve-thirty.

EUGENE. What time is it?

STAN. Twenty-five to one. We overslept.

EUGENE. Five minutes! You're yelling about five minutes?

STAN. (*hopping around the room, slapping his face*) Come on! Get up! If we fall asleep again, we're dead. Get your blood going. Move! Get Oxygen into your brains.

EUGENE. (*sitting up*) Don't slap me. My brains are up.

STAN. Read back what we have.

EUGENE. The whole thing?

STAN. From the beginning.

EUGENE. (flipping through the pads) We don't have anything.

STAN. Read the stuff we crossed out.

EUGENE. It's all crossed out.

STAN. Read it anyway. If I hear it again, then I'll know why it was wrong. Then we can get it right.

EUGENE. There's three pads of it. We'll spend an hour reading back what took us four hours to write what we didn't like.

STAN. Stop fighting me all the time. The more you fight me, the more pressure I feel. I need my head clear, I don't need it full of pressure. Just read it, will you, please!

EUGENE. (*reading from the first pad*) "A bedroom, about midnight. It is February and we see frost on the windows. One of the windows is open and we see the curtain blowing in. We hear teeth chattering from the bed . . . "

STAN. I can't hear it! I can't concentrate! I can't focus on anything! . . . Can you hear it?

EUGENE. Yeah, but I'm sitting a lot closer to me.

STAN. Let me talk to myself for a minute. (*He walks to a corner of the room.*) Stop it, Stanley! Stop and listen to what he's reading. You've waited your whole life for this, don't be a schmuck. (*He takes a deep breath and turns back to EUGENE.*) Okay. Read the rest.

EUGENE. (*reading from the first pad*) "A woman speaks. Her name is Shirley. Shirley says — (*He squints at the page.*) I can't read it. The rest is crossed out.

STAN. (*taking the pad from EUGENE*) Let me see it. (*He looks at the pad.*) What did you black it out for? When you cross something out, you just put a line through it. (*pointing a finger at EUGENE*) *Never* black out anything anymore, do you hear me? I want a thin, simple line.

EUGENE. You want me to take a drawing class?

STAN. Let's get another idea. If we're stuck this long, there must be something wrong with it.

EUGENE. It's going to take just as long to get another idea.

STAN. My head is tightening up. I'm all constricted inside. I just can't think. (*He thinks, then looks at EUGENE.*) This is hard, Gene. Really hard.

EUGENE. I know.

STAN. I won't give up if you don't give up.

EUGENE. I won't give up.

STAN. I love being a writer.

EUGENE. Me, too.

STAN. It's just the writing that's hard . . . You know what I mean?

EUGENE. Yeah.

STAN. Maybe I could be a re-writer . . . I'm terrific at fixing up things that are already written.

EUGENE. Like an editor. Every writer needs an editor.

STAN. . . . I don't want to hold you back, Gene. If

we don't come up with this sketch, if we don't get this job, I don't want it to stop you.

EUGENE. We'll come up with it. You just have to relax.

STAN. Because there are two writers I know. Marvin Rose and Alan Zweicker. They wrote something for Milton Berle once. They would take you on if I asked them.

EUGENE. Don't ask them. I don't want to write with someone else.

STAN. No, they're really good. Not as good as us, but you could at least make a living with them.

EUGENE. If they're not as good as us, what are we stopping for?

STAN. We're not stopping. I'm just planning ahead. Like I do in gin rummy . . . We could be the greatest, Gene. The greatest comedy writers in America . . . I just have to learn to deal with the pressure.

EUGENE. So do I. It's not easy for me either.

STAN. I'm feeling better. I'm glad we had this talk. It reassures me that you want to stick with me. I'm feeling more relaxed now.

EUGENE. So am I.

STAN. . . . Now if we can just get an idea.

EUGENE. We will. I know we will.

STAN. (*looking up*) Oh, God. Give us an idea, God! I'm here, God. Tell it to me. Give us an idea for a sketch you're not using. Tell me an idea that makes you laugh. (*EUGENE looks up to see if God is going to do it.*)

(*The Curtain Falls End of ACT I*

ACT TWO

*One month later. A few minutes before 6:00 p.m. on a
Saturday night. It is dark outside and snow is even
higher than before. It's a rough winter.
EUGENE is sitting up in bed in pajamas, robe, slippers
and white sweat socks. His desk chair serves as a
night table and on it are medicine and orange juice.
He wipes his nose with an old handkerchief.*

EUGENE. (*to audience*) It was the biggest night of my
life and here I was, sick in bed. I took Josie ice skating at
Rockefeller Center and fell down seven times and came
home with a 102 temperature. Jewish guys are never
good at sports played between November and April.

(*STAN leaves his bedroom and comes downstairs. He
looks out the front window toward the subway, then
sets about rearranging the furniture, the better to
hear the radio. KATE enters from the kitchen and
puts some festive doilies on the dining table.*)

EUGENE. (*continued*). . . . We came in with a finished sketch a few days late and although C.B.S. didn't
think we were ready for big-time television, they did put
us on small-time radio. Saturday night at six o'clock,
when everyone's getting dressed or eating dinner, but not
listening to C.B.S. radio. It was an experimental comedy
show to develop new talent and there were six young
writers. We knew our future was on the line that night,
but it wasn't C.B.S. we were worried about. It was Mom
and Pop's approval that meant the most to us. (*STAN*

56

brings a dining chair next to the sofa as KATE enters from the kitchen with a bowl of fruit and a bowl of nuts.)

STAN. No, MA!! No fruit! No nuts! No food at all.

KATE. Why not?

STAN. You want a room full of people eating cashew nuts? They won't hear *any*thing!

KATE. They could eat fruit. Bananas and oranges don't make noise. (*She puts the fruit on the table.*)

STAN. (*looks at his watch, then dashes to the front door*) Nine minutes to six and Pop's not home. I don't believe it. Of all nights in the world.

KATE. (*going to the foot of the stairs*) I don't know what to do about Eugene. He shouldn't be coming downstairs with the flu.

STAN. He'd be down here with leprosy. We'd pile up the pieces in a chair next to the radio. You think he's going to miss this? (*KATE goes to the breakfront and takes out candlesticks, which she puts on the table.*) Where's Grandpa? Did you call him?

KATE. He's taking his nap. I'll wake him just before it goes on.

STAN. We've got nine minutes!! It takes him twelve minutes to get his slippers on. (*calling up the stairs*) GRANDPA!! . . . Come on down! The show is on!!

KATE. (*returning the dining chair to its proper spot*) What kind of cookies do you want with the tea?

STAN. NO TEA! NO COOKIES!! . . . That's all I need is rattling cups and you saying, "Watch your crumbs."

KATE. (*entering the kitchen*) I was doing it for you, not for me.

STAN. Then don't do it for me. I want it quiet so you can hear the laughs. (*He turns on the radio.*) What's the matter with the radio? Is it plugged in? (*He looks behind the radio. KATE brings a tray of teacups from the kitchen to the breakfront.*) The radio is broken. I can't believe THE RADIO IS BROKEN!!

KATE. You have to let it warm up first.

STAN. It never takes this long. NO, NO, NO!! IT'S BROKEN!! (*He throws himself on the floor. The radio comes on. We hear dance music.*)

KATE. You see!

STAN. (*going to the radio to fine-tune it*) Is that clear? That doesn't sound clear to me. Can you hear it?

KATE. I hear it fine.

STAN. It's all the ice on the wires. I hate the winter.

KATE. (*coming to STAN at the radio*) You're going to get an ulcer, Stanley. You were never this nervous at Abraham and Straus.

STAN. Because no one tuned in to listen to me selling boy's clothing. (*He turns off the radio, then crosses to the front door and looks out.*) I don't see Pop. I don't even hear the train.

KATE. (*joining STAN at the front door*) You told him six o'clock?

STAN. Five hundred times. I pinned it on his pajamas last night. Where could he be?

KATE. I don't know. I'll go wake up Grandpa.

STAN. I'll do it. You turn off the tea. It'll start to whistle in the middle of the program.

(*KATE goes into the kitchen. STAN opens the front door and steps out into the cold, looking for his father. Then he comes back in and starts up the stairs.*)

EUGENE. (*sneezes; then, to audience:*) Mom and Pop were still together, but you'd never notice it. Almost a month had gone by since the big fight and they barely spoke to each other. And when they did speak, they spoke in the third person. "Is he coming home for dinner tonight?" "He's not sure. He'll let her know." "She doesn't care. Let him do what he wants." I kept looking around to see if there was another couple there.

STAN. (*opening EUGENE's bedroom door*) Let's go. We're on the air. (*knocking on BEN's door*) Grandpa! Come on. This is it! Gene and I are going to become Capitalists! (*to EUGENE, as they come downstairs*) Pop's not home yet.

EUGENE. You're kidding.

STAN. (*coming into the living room and again putting the dining chair next to the sofa*) This is some audience we've got. A mother who doesn't talk to a father who hasn't come home yet, and a grandfather who hasn't laughed since the stock market crashed.

EUGENE. (*coming slowly down the stairs*) My hair hurts. My pajamas hurt.

KATE. (*going to the foot of the stairs and holding up her hand for EUGENE to put his forehead on*) You have a hundred and two fever. (*She returns the dining chair to its proper place.*)

EUGENE. Why did they waste years developing the thermometer? You could make a fortune just feeling people in hospitals.

(*BEN comes down the stairs. EUGENE sits in the armchair. In the distance we hear the subway, and STAN comes running out of the kitchen to the front door.*)

STAN. There's the train. (*looks at his watch*) Even if he runs, he'll never make it on time.

BEN. (*at the foot of the stairs*) Have I got time to go to the bathroom?

STAN. We're on in three minutes.

KATE. (*to BEN*) You go when you have to go. Go on.

BEN. You got today's paper?

STAN. The *paper?* We won't see you till Tuesday! (*more reasonably*) Didn't I hear you in the bathroom five minutes ago, Gramps?

BEN. Was that me? Your right. Forget it. I don't have to go.

STAN. (*seeing EUGENE in the armchair*) Not there. That's Pop's chair. Sit over there.

KATE. (*seeing EUGENE about to sit on the sofa*) Not there. There's always a draft in that spot.

BEN. (*seeing EUGENE about to sit on the other end of the sofa*) Let me sit there. I have to put my feet up. They're swollen again.

EUGENE. (*standing in the middle of the living room*) Boy, this is the toughest seat in town to get. (*KATE pushes a dining chair next to the sofa for EUGENE, then puts some pillows under BEN's head.*)

STAN. (*looking out the front windows*) There's a few people getting off. It's so dark. I can't make out anyone.

BEN. (*stretching out on the sofa; to EUGENE:*) So, what kind of a story is this?

EUGENE. It's not a story. It's a variety show. It's music and sketches and monologues and comedy interviews. It's entertainment.

BEN. Why, because they have nothing to say?

EUGENE. It's not *supposed* to say anything.

BEN. There's nothing to say? With three-quarters of the world in economic slavery, there's nothing to say?

STAN. (*sitting in the armchair*) They didn't want any sketches on economic slavery, Grandpa. They're looking for laughs, not an uprising.

KATE. (*taking her knitting from the breakfront*) There's nothing wrong with a good laugh. We could all use a good laugh these days.

EUGENE. What time is it?

STAN. (*looking at his watch*) Jesus! It's almost on. And he's not home yet. (*He goes to the front door and looks out.*)

EUGENE. God, my heart is pounding.

KATE. (*taking dates from the breakfront*) Does anyone want some dates? Dates don't make noise. (*She gives a date to BEN, then sits in the armchair.*)

STAN. NO, MA! Nobody wants anything.

EUGENE. Please, God, don't let us be humiliated.

KATE. Aunt Blanche has all her friends listening. Grandma has everybody in her apartment in Miami . . . Everybody in Brighton Beach is tuned in.

BEN. But try to get them to read a newspaper, they're too busy.

STAN. (*At the radio, adjusting the volume, the "Chubby Waters Show" theme music comes on.*) Shhh! Here it comes! This is it!

EUGENE. Good luck, Stan.

STAN. (*going to EUGENE, shaking his hand, then coming back to sit in front of the radio*) Good luck, Eug!

(*From the radio, after the theme music, we hear the announcer.*)

ANNOUNCER. From New York City, The Columbia Broadcasting System presents, "The Chubby Waters Show," starring Chubby Waters and featuring Fred C. Sherman, Grace Dooley, Don Paloma, Sarah Mac-Laren, John Dunninger, Dick Ambrose and his Waldorf-Astoria Orchestra and special guest star, Pepito, the only Spanish-Speaking Dog in the English-Speaking World.

(*The theme music continues under the following:*)

BEN. (*to EUGENE*) They have a Spanish-speaking dog?

EUGENE. Wait'll you hear him. He's hysterical.

BEN. He really speaks Spanish, or they taught it to him?

STAN. He can bark, "Si, si." Whatever you ask him, he says, "Si, si."

BEN. (*to STAN and KATE*) If he speaks Spanish, the audience won't understand. They're not as smart as the dog.

KATE. Why didn't they say your names?

EUGENE. At the end of the program . . . if they have time. Shh. It's on again.

ANNOUNCER. (*from the radio*) And now, the star of "The Chubby Waters Show," Mr. Chubby Waters. (*The studio audience applauds.*)

KATE. (*to STAN, whose head is pressed to the radio grillwork*) Get your head away from there, Stanley. You'll go deaf.

CHUBBY. (*from the radio*) Thank you. Thank you, ladies and gentlemen . . . I'm kinda nervous, this being my first big-time New York program. I'm from Decatur, Illinois, and our humor is a lot slower out there . . . I had my own program in Decatur and when I told a joke, they didn't laugh until next week's show. (*The studio audience laughs.*)

BEN. Oi vay!

CHUBBY. Decatur's kind of a small town. I'll tell you

how small it is. Some guys drove through town and threw a snowball at us . . . and we were shoveling it out for a week. (*The studio audience laughs.*)

KATE. Did that really happen?

EUGENE. No, Ma. It's just a joke.

STAN. Shhh, will you please.

CHUBBY. Decatur's sort of an agricultural town. We sell all the fruit and vegetables that drop offa trucks passing through. (*The studio audience laughs.*)

BEN. Only in America this man makes a living.

STAN. (*to BEN*) Are you going to do this all night?

CHUBBY. The census taker told us the average family in Decatur has about two and a half children. Most families prefer to have two girls and half a boy. (*The studio audience laughs.*) The reason being that with half a girl, you still got to buy the whole dress, but with half a boy, you only got to buy the pants. (*The studio audience laughs and applauds.*)

BEN. (*to Eugene*) You wrote that?

EUGENE. No. One of the other guys.

BEN. Stay away from him. He's crazy.

STAN. Great. Can't even hear the program in my own house.

CHUBBY. When Abe Lincoln left Springfield, Illinois, his first speech was supposed to be in Decatur. But his legs were too long, and darned if he didn't step over us. (*The studio audience laughs.*)

BEN. In Russia, he'd be shot by now.

STAN. I can't believe this. My own grandfather.

CHUBBY. The folks back home are really rootin' for me. Because if I don't make good, I'll have to go back to Decatur, but a new baby was born there yesterday and well, I lost my space. (*The studio audience laughs.*)

KATE. Why is he telling us all this? (*STAN gets up and walks to the dining room to calm himself.*)

EUGENE. It's a monologue. He's warming up the audience.

BEN. They'd be better off sending up heat.

CHUBBY. 'Preciate meetin' ya. I'll be right back when I make my first tour through New York City and meet the Pitkin family of Coney Island, Brooklyn, New York.

STAN. That's ours! Ours is next. (*Dick Ambrose and his orchestra plays over the radio. The front door opens, and JACK rushes in.*) Pop! You just made it! You're just in time! Our sketch is next. (*KATE gets up from the armchair and goes to the dining table and her knitting. STAN helps JACK off with his coat.*)

JACK. I'm sorry I'm late. I couldn't help it.

EUGENE. It's okay. You didn't miss anything. You timed it on the button.

STAN. Sit in the armchair, Pop. You can hear perfectly.

JACK. Three trains were frozen to the tracks. It's some mess out there.

STAN. (*ushering JACK to the armchair, and then sitting in front of the radio*) Sit down, Pop . . . The comedian's name is Chubby Waters . . . He's a little corny, but the network likes that.

EUGENE. He's about to visit the Pitkin family from Coney Island. That's ours.

KATE. Does he want anything to eat?

JACK. He'll take something after . . . Thank her anyway.

EUGENE. (*to audience*) You're not going to get big laughs from people who call each other "him" and "her"! (*Dick Ambrose and his orchestra finish. The studio audience applauds.*)

ANNOUNCER. (*from the radio*) . . . Newly arrived in New York, Mr. Charles "Chubby" Waters, decides to visit the city he's always dreamed of, ever since he was born half a child in Decatur, Illinois.

STAN. (*to JACK*) I'll explain that later, Pop.

ANNOUNCER. But it's not the Empire State or the Statue of Liberty or Grant's Tomb that Mr. Waters wants to see. It's the people; for it's the people who make our cities great. And so he decided to take the subway. Being half a person, he walks under the turnstile and rides out to Coney Island. He gets off, smelling the fresh sea water and the stale frankfurter rolls, and walks through the historic streets . . . and rings the bell of Mr. and Mrs. Morris Pitkin. (*We hear a doorbell ring*)

EUGENE. (*to BEN*) That's sound effects. (*We hear a door open.*)

MRS. PITKIN. (*from the radio*) Yes?

CHUBBY. (*from the radio*) How do you do? My name is Chubby Waters. May I ask, have you ever heard of me?

MRS. PITKIN. Not that I heard of. (*a small laugh from the studio audience*)

CHUBBY. Well, I'm a radio comedian, and I have a brand new show on C.B.S. starting this Saturday night at six. Will you be listening to it?

MRS. PITKIN. Only if *you* can make a pot roast. (*a bigger laugh from the studio audience*)

CHUBBY. Is that anything like a roast ham?

MRS. PITKIN. Not in *this* neighborhood. (*a big studio laugh*)

CHUBBY. I'm trying to familiarize myself with New Yorkers, and I wondered if I could come in and say hello to your family.

MRS. PITKIN. Why? My *family* doesn't say hello to my family. (*studio laugh*)

CHUBBY. I don't mean to impose, but it would be very helpful to me. I'd be most grateful.

MRS. PITKIN. Alright . . . Wipe your feet.

CHUBBY. Certainly. (*sound effect of wiping feet*) . . . There! They're clean.

MRS. PITKIN. Your *shoes* are clean. I meant the *feet.* Take your socks off too. (*studio laugh*)

CHUBBY. Certainly . . . There! Now everything's clean . . . Oh, what a pretty house. I like your furniture. What style would you call it?

MRS. PITKIN. Sacrifice! That's what you have to do to get it. (*studio laugh*)

KATE. She reminds me of someone, but I can't think who.

CHUBBY. Is that a new rug?

MRS. PITKIN. Where?

CHUBBY. That thing rolled up in the corner.

MRS. PITKIN. No. That's my father-in-law. (*studio laugh*)

CHUBBY. He sleeps on the floor?

MRS. PITKIN. He likes to sleep on newspapers, because if he wakes up in the middle of the night, he's got something to read. (*studio laugh*)

CHUBBY. A well-red bed . . .

MRS. PITKIN. Step over the papers, please. If you get print on your bare feet, it'll be all over my father-in-law. (*studio laugh*)

CHUBBY. I'll put my socks back on . . . Is it possible to meet your husband?

MRS. PITKIN. Sure. Do what I do. Write in for an appointment. (*studio laugh*) He's in here. But be quiet. He's working.

CHUBBY. What does he do?

MRS. PITKIN. He's in ladies' pajamas. (*studio laugh*)

CHUBBY. How do you feel about your husband being in ladies' pajamas?

MRS. PITKIN. That's the sacrifice I had to make to get the furniture. (*Big studio laugh and applause. The sound of the radio show becomes muted, almost inaudible, they all listen, except EUGENE, who turns to the audience.*)

EUGENE. . . . Practically everything we wrote scored a bull's-eye . . . The only sad note was that, although we were a smash at C.B.S., we came up real short in the living room in Brighton Beach . . . The thirty minutes went by about as quickly as the Middle Ages . . . Finally, our agony was over. (*The sound of the radio show comes up again. The theme music is playing at a fast tempo and we hear the ANNOUNCER rattling off the credits.*)

ANNOUNCER. "The Chubby Waters Show" was a Steve Coleman-Mel Jason Production in association with the Columbia Broadcasting System . . . Pepito, the talking dog, appeared through the courtesy of R.K.O. Pictures . . . The producer of "The Chubby Waters Show" is Jeff Bishop, directed by Todd Allen and written by Michael Solomon, Larry Shapiro, Frank Connally, Donald Kreiss and Stanley and Eugene Gerard.

STAN. (*as he and EUGENE look dumbfounded at the radio*) JEROME!!!

ANNOUNCER. Good night from New York to all of you from all of us. (*STANLEY switches off the radio.*)

STAN. (*shouting at the radio*) You couldn't even remember "Jerome," you stupid idiot! (*storming into the dining room*) Gerard doesn't even sound like Jerome. I'm calling a lawyer. I should have been at rehearsals.

EUGENE. It was a great audience, though, wasn't it?

STAN. We got through it, Eug. At least we got through it. (*The boys stare at KATE.*)

KATE. Well, I liked it. It was lively. The actors were good. Everybody remembered their lines.

STAN. It's radio, Ma. They read them from scripts.

EUGENE. (*returning his dining chair to the table*) But did you really, really like it, Ma?

KATE. What do you mean, did I like it? Didn't you hear the audience laughing?

EUGENE. That was them, not you.

KATE. (*going to the closet for her coat*) There were too many funny lines. They came so fast, I couldn't find a place to laugh. Next week make it slower.

STAN. Where are you going?

KATE. I have to go next door to Mrs. Slutsky's to borrow some honey for this one's tea. (*kissing EU-GENE*) I'm very proud of both of you. (*She kisses STAN.*)

STAN. I can go.

KATE. You have a date in half an hour, don't you? It's worth it for me to catch a cold to see you get married. (*She exits through the back door. The boys turn their gaze on BEN.*)

BEN. (*rising slowly*) I'm going to finish my nap.

STAN. You didn't like it. I can tell.

BEN. (*crossing toward the stairs*) I didn't hate it either. When I don't hate something, it's not bad.

EUGENE. What was wrong with it?

BEN. To me, comedy has to have a point. What was the point of this?

EUGENE. To make people laugh.

BEN. That's not a point. To make people *aware,* that's a point. Political satire, that's what you should have written. You could change half the world with political satire. Think about that some time.

EUGENE. Political satire? We're lucky we came up with a few good jokes.

BEN. (*on the stairs*) I'll teach you how to write it. You

sneak in a few remarks about what's wrong with this political system. If you make it funny enough, C.B.S. will never notice.

EUGENE. (*to STAN*) Can't you just see it? . . . "The Socialist Revue" starring Chubby Trotsky . . . We'd be writing it from jail.

BEN. I liked the Talking Dog. "Si, si!" He didn't make any points, but he made me laugh. "Si, si!" (*BEN continues up the stairs and to his bedroom.*)

STAN. You haven't said anything yet, Pop. Is anything wrong?

JACK. I tell you the truth, I had a hard time listening.

EUGENE. Why?

JACK. Sit down. Both of you. (*They sit on the sofa.*) That was us you were writing about tonight, wasn't it? The family.

STAN. No. Not really.

JACK. Not really? You don't think you made fun of this family tonight?

STAN. (*after a look to EUGENE*) No. We weren't thinking of the family. It's all the people we know. Here in Brighton Beach or Coney Island or Brooklyn. People we grew up with. It's no one particular.

JACK. I'm willing to give you the benefit of the doubt. But listen: The woman says to the man, "My family doesn't say hello to my family." That wasn't your mother? If that wasn't your mother, who was it?

EUGENE. It's every mother who lives out here. They all talk like that. That's what happens in neighborhoods. Everyone sounds alike.

JACK. Everyone in this area knows about your grandfather. He falls asleep on buses, on trains, in the library. So you have a grandfather on the show who falls asleep on newspapers on the floor. The people out here who are listening know who you're talking about. And you're not ashamed to put a thing like that on the radio?

STAN. He heard it. He didn't say a word. He never thought it was him.

JACK. I don't care if he said a word or not. *I* knew it was him and *you* knew it was him. It makes no difference who he thought it was. You don't poke fun of your own grandfather in front of the whole world. (*He takes his rubbers to the closet.*)

EUGENE. We'd never poke fun at him. We love Grandpa. But old people fall asleep a lot so we just wrote it down. It's just a coincidence.

JACK. (*pacing angrily*) And what about her husband? What did you say about him on the radio?

STAN. Nothing? . . . Eugene, on the program, what does the woman say her husband does for a living?

EUGENE. He's in ladies' pajamas.

JACK. And I'm in ladies' raincoats, right?

EUGENE. A man being in ladies' pajamas just sounds funny. It's a joke.

JACK. Are you going to pretend you don't know what's going on between your mother and me? . . . Heh? . . . You're not deaf, your're not blind, so you must know something, right? (*The boys say nothing.*) I don't know what she tells you. I don't know what stories she fills your head with. God knows what she must say to you about me.

STAN. She never said anything to me, I swear.

JACK. But you know what's going on, don't you?

STAN. In a house with walls like this, you know everything.

JACK. Well, I'll tell you something else. Not only do these walls have ears, the walls on the house next door have them, and the house next to that one have them . . . The whole damn neighborhood has them . . . In a community like this, everybody knows everybody else's business . . . So what do you think happens when the people in Brighton Beach hear a radio program with a woman on it who sounds familiar, tell us her husband's in ladies' pajamas—and they know what that means—they understand the innuendo . . . when they hear that on the radio, what are they thinking when they know that the two sons of the man in ladies' pajamas wrote the program? . . . Heh? . . . Tell me what they're thinking.

EUGENE. I know what you're getting at, but I don't think that's what's going to happen.

JACK. Can you promise me that? Can you give a written guarantee? . . . The only thing people like better than gossip is hearing filth, and that's what those people heard on the radio tonight.

STAN. (rising) What are you talking about? That's crazy.

JACK. I will never forgive either one of you for ridiculing me in front of my neighbors, in front of my friends, in front of strangers. You'll never know how many people I called to tell to turn on the program because I was so proud of my two sons. That's a mistake I won't make again.

STAN. You may have been proud to *them,* but you never encouraged *us.* If it were up to you, I'd still be selling boys' clothing.

JACK. After what I heard tonight, I wish to God you were.

EUGENE. Stan, stop it! Cut it out! . . . I'm sorry you feel this way, Pop. We both are. But I swear, we never thought of you and Mom when we wrote the sketch. We just thought of older couples who lived in this neighborhood, but when it got down on paper, I guess it sounded like the ones we knew best . . . It wasn't intentional, I swear. (*STAN sits in the armchair. JACK sits between the two boys, but talks to STAN.*)

JACK. You know what I thought when I heard it? I swear to God. I thought it was their way of getting back at me for hurting their mother . . . Is that so impossible to imagine?

STAN. No. Not so impossible.

JACK. Ah, maybe we're getting closer to the truth now . . . What did she tell you about this woman? Did she tell you what she was like?

STAN. I told you. She never talked to me about any of it.

JACK. But you seem to have feelings about it. Where did you get them from? Someone you know from New York? You have lots of friends there, right? Because let me tell you something . . . No matter what you heard about this woman, you will never find a kinder or more decent human being on this earth. You understand me?

STAN. Go to hell.

JACK. What did you say to me?

STAN. I said, "Go to hell!"

EUGENE. Stan. Please. Don't do this.

STAN. (*standing*) I don't care if she's Joan of Arc, that's still my mother we're talking about. Do whatever you God damn please, but don't blame Gene and me of humiliating you when you're the one who's been humiliating *us* . . . You're so damn guilty for what you've done, you're accusing everyone else of betraying *you* . . . I never wanted to hear what was happening to you and Mom. I prayed every night you would both work it out and it would pass out of our lives. You could have called each other "him" and "her" forever as long as it kept you together . . . All my life you taught me about things like dignity and principles and I believed them. I still do, I guess . . . But what kind of principles does a man have when he tells his sons the woman he's seeing on the side is a wonderufl, decent human being?

JACK. (*stands, composes himself, then walks slowly to STAN*) Either you've grown up too fast . . . or I've outlived my place in this house. (*JACK looks at both boys, then goes up the stairs to his bedroom and closes the door.*)

EUGENE. (*begins to fold the afghan*) Jesus! I don't believe what just happened . . . I'm shaking, I swear to God.

STAN. Do you think what I said was wrong?

EUGENE. No. I just don't know if you should have said it.

STAN. I didn't bring the subject up, did I? I never accused him of anything. Every one of my friends' fathers screwed around *some*times. Maybe *all* the time. But they don't ask their sons to take the woman into the family.

EUGENE. He didn't say it like that.

STAN. Screw you, Eugene. What are you taking *his* side for? What are you going to do, buy her a Mother's Day present?

EUGENE. I'm not taking his side. Something's happened to him these last few years, I know that. But you don't know his side. You don't know the whole story.

STAN. He didn't listen to one word we wrote on that program. He's so paranoid, he thinks it was all about him. Jesus, the one night in our life we wanted his approval, and all he does is tell us what shits we are . . . "Maybe I've outlived this house," he says . . . Is that our fault, too? Another truckload of guilt dumped at our feet . . . He can have the God damned house because I'm getting out. The both of us. (*He goes to sit beside EUGENE on the sofa.*) It's time to move, Gene. This is no place for us. We've been waiting for a chance to leave, this is it. They liked our work at C.B.S., we can afford a place in New York. We should go, Gene, and we should go soon. (*EUGENE stares at him.*) If you don't come, I'll go alone.

EUGENE. No. You're right. I think we should go . . . I just wish it didn't have to be when everything's so bad here.

STAN. There's two or three places I saw. One over on the West Side with a little back yard that gets the sun. Great place for parties. It'll be better for us, Eug. You'll be able to see your girlfriend more often. You'll have your own room, she'll be able to stay overnight.

EUGENE. No. She's not that kind.

STAN. Well, you can bring over the kind that do and take your girlfriend to the movies. (*STAN goes to straighten the armchair.*)

EUGENE. Stan? . . . When we were writing the sketch, did you think we were writing about Mom and Pop?

STAN. (*coming back to sit next to EUGENE*) No. It was like you said. It's everybody out here. I thought the father was Mr. Greenblatt . . . Joe Pinotti's grandfather once fell asleep in his oatmeal. He almost suffocated.

EUGENE. I did. I thought it was Mom and Pop. And Grandpa. They were the ones I was writing about.

STAN. Okay. So? It was a little bit of them, too.

EUGENE. No. It was only them. The joke about him being in ladies' pajamas . . . I didn't mean it the way he said. To me it was just a joke. But maybe I did it subconsciously the way Pop said.

STAN. If it's subconscious, it's not a crime, Eugene.

EUGENE. I was the one who should have had the fight with him. Only I didn't know I was so angry. Like there's part of my head that makes me this nice, likeable, funny kid . . . and there's the other part, the part that writes, that's an angry, hostile, real son of a bitch. (*The phone rings.*)

STAN. (*going to answer the phone*) Well, you'd better make friends with the son of a bitch, because he's the one who's going to make you a big living. (*into the phone*) Hello? . . . Joe? . . . Did you hear it? What'd you think? . . . Wait a minute, I have to tell Gene. (*turning to EUGENE*) Joe Pinotti still can't stop laughing. He though it was better than Jack Benny. (*back into the phone*) What? You're kidding . . . Wait a minute . . . (*to EUGENE*) His mother and father thought it was about them. They said it was so typical. They loved it. (*back into the phone*) What? . . . No, they were crazy about it here . . . Yeah, my father thought it was great.

(*KATE enters through the back door, carrying a jar of honey.*)

KATE. (*going to the closet to hang up her coat*) Who's that on the phone?

EUGENE. Joe Pinotti, Stan's friend. He loved the show.

KATE. Why shouldn't he? . . . Where's your father?

EUGENE. Up in his room . . . *Your* room.

KATE. (*picking up the tray of sandwiches from the dining table*) The program's over. You shouldn't be downstairs. Get back in bed.

EUGENE. Mom, I'm not eight years old.

KATE. You are until you move out of this house. (*She exits into the kitchen.*)

STAN. (*into the phone*) Can I quote you on that? . . . I'll talk to you tomorrow, Joe. Yeah . . . Thanks a lot. (*He hangs up the phone.*) The man sells kitchenware at Abraham and Straus. He should be the critic on *The New York Times.*

KATE. (*entering from the kitchen*) What did your father think of the show?

EUGENE. (*crossing to the stairs*) He thought it was very lifelike.

STAN. He'll probably tell you later.

KATE. He tells me hello and good-bye, that's what he tells me. Hurry up and get dressed. Don't keep a girl waiting. (*KATE exits into the kitchen with a tray of cups and saucers. EUGENE and STAN go into EUGENE's room.*)

STAN. I don't get it. How can they sleep in the same bed night after night for a month and not say a word to each other?

EUGENE. I wonder if they say "Gezundheit" if the other one sneezes.

STAN. Jerry Applebaum told me his mother and father didn't talk to each other for over a year, and they still made love three times a week. (*STAN goes into his own room*)

EUGENE. That's more times than most people who talk to each other. (*STAN dresses for his date. EUGENE turns to the audience.*) If I ever married Josie, that would never happen to us. How could I sleep in the same bed with her without touching her skin and stroking her hair and telling her how much I love her? Then again, maybe that's what my father said before he married my mother.

STAN. (*coming into EUGENE's room*) How do I look?

EUGENE. Like a Jewish Cary Grant. (*The phone rings.*)

STAN. I've been after this girl for six months, but to-night's the night, kid.

EUGENE. How do you know?

STAN. She loves celebrities. (*STAN goes downstairs, as KATE comes out of the kitchen to answer the phone.*) Get a good night's sleep. We've got a show to write tomorrow morning.

KATE. Not if he's still sick. (*She picks up the phone.*) Hello? . . . Who's this? . . . Momma? Oh, my God! I didn't recognize you. You sound wonderful . . . you sound younger.

EUGENE. (*comes out of his room and calls from top of the stairs*) Is that Josie?

KATE. It's not Josie. Go to bed. (*back into phone*) No, Momma, it's Eugene. (*STAN kisses KATE on the cheek, and exits through the front door.*)

EUGENE. Ask her if she heard the show.

KATE. (*into phone*) So, did you make any friends? . . . Uh   huh . . . Uh   huh . . . Uh huh . . . Momma, you don't have to name them all, I'm glad you made friends.

EUGENE. Ask her if she heard the show.

KATE. Did you hear the radio show? . . . Eugene and Stanley's . . .

EUGENE. Did she like it?

KATE. (*to EUGENE*) She loved it.

EUGENE. Really?

KATE. (*into phone*) You know *who?* . . . The Pitkin family in Coney Island?

EUGENE. Oh, my God!

KATE. No, Momma. They're actors . . . He's not a dentist. That's a different family . . . These are *actors* . . . Alright, Momma. I won't argue with you. If you know them, you know them. (*She shrugs to EUGENE.*) Yes. Everyone else is fine . . . Jack is doing very well . . . Blanche told you what? . . . No, no. That was months ago. Well, I'm telling you different . . . It's fine . . . (*looks at EUGENE, who is sitting on the steps*) What are you sitting there for? I told you to get to bed. (*He moves slowly up the steps, then stops to listen.*) . . . Yes. I know you haven't heard from Poppa . . . He's been very busy. He asks for you all the time . . . No. In his room.

EUGENE. You want me to get him?

KATE. (*waving at him to keep quiet*) Momma, let it alone . . . I don't think it's a good idea . . . When he's ready to call you, he'll call you . . . I don't think he means to hurt you. He just has to do things in his own way . . . Listen, you told me once yourself. Men are peculiar . . . I'm not defending him, Momma . . . Where am I taking his side? I told him not to go to Florida? . . . Who told you that? . . . *Who told you that?* . . . I'm not yelling at you, but don't accuse me of what you make up in your own head . . . I didn't say — alright. I'm sorry . . . I said I'm sorry . . . Alright, Momma . . . Yes . . . Yes . . . I know you do . . . I do too . . . Goodbye, Momma . . . I'll call you next — (*But Momma's clicked off. KATE stands there with the phone in her hand. Then replaces it, wiping the receiver clean. She crosses to the breakfront and puts away the flatware. EUGENE watches her.*)

EUGENE. How about if I made you one of my famous chocolate milkshakes?

KATE. You put too much Hershey's in it. I don't like it so sweet.

EUGENE. (*coming downstairs, to KATE*) You know what I thought?

KATE. What?

EUGENE. I thought when you grew up, you stopped having trouble with your parents.

KATE. Yeah? Then be thankful you're still young. (*She goes into the kitchen. EUGENE thinks about this for a moment, then looks in at KATE in the kitchen.*)

EUGENE. I never see you stop working. When Stanley and I make enough money, we're going to get you a maid, Ma.

KATE. A maid? In Brighton Beach? People would pay admission to come over and look at her. (*EUGENE sits on the corner of the dining table. KATE comes out of the kitchen with a cup of tea.*) Oh, my God! Get off that table! (*She whacks him with a dish towel.*) Are you crazy, sitting on my dining room table?

EUGENE. (*jumping off the table*) I'm sorry. I didn't leave any marks.

KATE. Marks I can clean off. But I never want to see you show disrespect to this table.

EUGENE. I didn't mean it . . . I'm sorry, table. I apologize. (*She glares at him.*) Is it so expensive?

KATE. My grandfather made this table. With his own hands. For my grandmother . . . (*She stirs honey into the tea, then motions for him to sit and drink it.*) Over fifty-two years she had this table . . . When I was a little girl, I'd go to her house and she'd let me help her polish it . . . I didn't know it was work. I thought it was fun . . . Maybe because she and I did it together . . . I was closer to her than I was to my own mother . . . Is that a terrible thing to say?

EUGENE. Not if that's how you felt.

KATE. (*clearing fruit, candlestick and doilies from the*

table) When she died, she left a will. She gave away jewelry, dresses, even a little cash. But she knew what I wanted. (*She looks at the table.*) The table you eat on means everything. It's the one time in the day the whole family is together . . . This is where you share things . . . People who eat out all the time don't get to be a family . . . (*She sits at the table.*) When I'm gone, if you and your Josie get married, this will be your table.

EUGENE. What about Stanley?

KATE. Stanley won't get married so fast. And when he does, you make sure he brings his family to eat at your house.

EUGENE. Maybe you'll let me polish it with you one day.

KATE. When your wife has a little girl, send *her* over. She and I will polish it. (*She collects EUGENE's teacup, and goes into the kitchen.*)

EUGENE. (*calling into the kitchen*) Maybe we'll have twins. You can polish it twice as fast. (*KATE re-enters with furniture polish and a rag. She begins to wipe off the table, with EUGENE following closely.*)

KATE. Don't follow me around like that. You make me nervous.

EUGENE. (*retreating to the breakfront*) I'm not following you. I just feel like talking to you . . . I love it when you tell me about the old days.

KATE. I don't remember them anymore. They were such a long time ago.

EUGENE. You just told me about the dining room table, and *that* was a long time ago . . . What was your grandmother like?

KATE. (*stops wiping the table for a moment*) Tiny. Little bit of a thing. All the women were small in those days. When I was nine years old, I was bigger than she was . . . My grandfather had to pick her up to see the Statue of Liberty.

EUGENE. That must have been some day.

KATE. This is what they dreamed of. Their whole life. To get to America. And when they saw that statue, they started to cry. The women were wailing, the men were shaking, everybody praying. You know why?

EUGENE. Because they were free.

KATE. Because they took one look at that statue and said, "That's not a Jewish woman. We're going to have problems again." (*She goes back to polishing the table.*)

EUGENE. That would be a riot. A Jewish Statue of Liberty. In her left hand, she'd be holding a baking pan . . . and in the right hand, held up high, the electric bill.

KATE. And my grandfather, of course, was a Socialist. When *he* saw the statue he said, "It's too big. They should have made a small one and given the money to people who needed it."

EUGENE. If your whole family were Socialists, Ma, how come you're not?

KATE. Not the whole family. Just the men . . . A man doesn't fight for political causes on an empty stomach.

EUGENE. But you vote. You voted for President Roosevelt.

KATE. I liked his face. I trusted him. I got nervous that he smoked with a cigarette holder, that was a little fancy for me . . . But he had polio. And I figured a man who walked with crutches wasn't out to take advantage of poor people.

EUGENE. You amaze me sometimes.

KATE. And I like Harry Truman. Him I trust, too.

EUGENE. Why?

KATE. Because he walks everywhere. Seven o'clock in the morning, he's out walking the streets. The Secret Service men can't even keep up with him . . . He was once a haberdasher, did you know that? And a man who has to get up early in the morning in the winter to open up a store, knows what it's like to be a working man . . . Alright. That's enough already. I want you in bed. (*She has finished polishing and takes the rag and bottle into the kitchen.*)

EUGENE. I will. In a few minutes. First tell me about George Raft.

KATE. (*coming out of the kitchen*) George Raft . . . If I tell you about George Raft again, you're going to tell me you still don't believe me. (*She takes the fruit bowl into the kitchen.*)

EUGENE. I believe you. I believe every word you say. So tell me how you met George Raft.

KATE. (*from the kitchen*) You heard it a hundred times.

EUGENE. (*putting the skein of yarn around his hands*) I know. But every time you tell it, it gets a little better. (*She enters from the kitchen, and sees him with the yarn. He pushes the ball of yarn toward her.*) Go on.

KATE. (*slowly taking up the ball of yarn and beginning to wind it*) The night I danced with him, I committed a sin. I knew God was going to punish me for it, and He did. You pay for your mistakes in this world.

EUGENE. What sin did you commit?

KATE. The day before I was going to the Primrose, my Aunt Sipra died. My mother's sister. The next morning, the whole family went to the funeral. I took the day off from work and that night we all sat at my grandmother's to sit in mourning . . . But I knew that night George Raft was coming to the Primrose. He was a friend of the owners and he promised he would come. I never dreamed he'd dance with me. I just wanted to watch him. But in the back of my head I thought, if he sees me dance, who knows, he might ask me to get up on the floor with him . . . He wasn't even an actor yet. Just this skinny kid who looked like Rudolph Valentino. But the best ballroom dancer in New York. And to dance with him made you Queen of the City.

EUGENE. Did he flip a coin like he does in the movies?

KATE. Never. But he always smoothed down his hair with his right hand. Every two minutes, smoothing his hair down. It got so shiny, you could see your face in it when you danced with him.

EUGENE. So you went to the dance that night.

KATE. (*forgetting the yarn and sitting*) I told my mother I wasn't feeling well. I told her I just threw up in the bathroom, which I didn't, so she sent me home. I knew she and Poppa and the girls wouldn't be home till midnight. So I ran home and changed my dress and went to the Primrose with my girlfriend, Adele Abrams. And all the time I knew that God was going to punish me for this . . . I kept saying to Adele on the way over, I wish I was a Catholic. Then I could go to church, confess my sins and God would forgive me. But I knew I just committed another sin by wishing I was Catholic . . . I was throwing my whole life away for this one night to see George Raft.

EUGENE. Did you have a—you know—a crush on him?

KATE. On George Raft? You think I'm crazy? He was Italian. I was in enough trouble already. He wasn't my type anyway . . . Your father was the one I had the crush on . . . Since I was thirteen years old. He was five years older than me. He went with a whole other crowd.

In those days young people didn't tell each other they had crushes on them. You had to guess. So you sent messages with your eyes, your face, the way you walked by them.

EUGENE. How did you walk by him?

KATE. Not too much, not too little. But he was hard to figure out. He was never a show-off, never a fancy Dan. He didn't smile a lot, but when he did, you knew he meant it. Most boys then smiled at everything. They thought it gave them a good personality. Jack was too honest to put on a good personality. He was what he was . . . and to get a smile from Jack Jerone, you knew you had to earn it . . . But it cost him plenty. The smilers got to be the salesmen. The smilers got to be the bosses. The smilers got all the girls. Your father paid the price for not being a phony . . . It was hard to impress him. That's why I went to the Primrose that night. I thought if Jack heard that I danced with George Raft, maybe I'd get him to notice me.

EUGENE. This is a movie. There's a whole movie in this story, Ma. And one day I'm going to write it.

KATE. So that night, in a pouring rain, me and Adele Abrams went to the Primrose. My hair got soaking wet, I lost my curls, I wanted to die. But then I got this brilliant idea. Instead of drying it, I combed it straight down and left it wet. Jet black hair. I looked like a Latin from Manhattan . . . The perfect partner for George Raft . . . When I walked out of the ladies' room, my own friends didn't recognize me.

EUGENE. I can't believe this is *my mother* you're talking about.

KATE. Don't worry. I knew God was going to punish me for the wet hair, too . . . Ten boys must have asked me to dance. But I said no to all of them because I didn't want to tire myself out . . . And then I started to get scared. Because it was ten after eleven and he still didn't show up. If I wasn't home by twelve, my parents would walk in and find out I was lying to them. And with my mother, I didn't need God to punish me.

EUGENE. Twelve o'clock! Cinderella! This story has everything.

KATE. And then, at twenty after eleven, he walks in . . . Like the King of Spain. My heart was beating louder than the drummer in the band . . . He had two friends with him, one on each side, like bodyguards. And I swear, there was something in their inside pockets. I thought to myself, they're either guns or more jars of grease for his hair.

EUGENE. (to audience) She actually had a sense of humor. This was a side of my mother I hardly ever saw. (to KATE) So, he walks in with these two guys.

KATE. (taking off her sweater and standing C.) So, he walks in with these two friends and I know I don't have much time. So I grabbed Bobby Zugetti, a shoe clerk, who was the best dancer at the Primrose, and said, "Bobby, dance with me!" . . . I knew he had a crush on me and I never gave him a tumble before. He didn't know what hit him. So out on the floor we go, and we fox-trotted from one side of the ballroom and back. In and out, bobbing and weaving through the crowd, gliding across the floor like a pair of ice skaters.

EUGENE. "Begin the Beguine" . . . Maybe "Night and Day." That's what I would use in the picture.

KATE. And I never once looked over to see if George Raft was looking at me . . . I wanted to get *his* attention, I didn't want to give him mine . . . The music finishes and Bobby dips me down to the floor. It was a little lower than a nice girl should dip, but I figured one more sin wouldn't kill me . . . And I walk over to Adele, I'm dripping with perspiration, and I said, "Well? Did he watch me?" . . . And she said, "It's hard to tell. His eyes don't move." . . . So I look over and he's sitting at a table with his two friends and Adele is right. His eyes don't move. And it's twenty-five to twelve, and he's never even noticed me. And I said to myself, "Well, if it's not meant to be, it's not meant to be." . . . and Adele and I started for the door.

EUGENE. The tension mounts. The audience is on the edge of their seats.

KATE. And as we pass their table, George Raft stands up and says, "Excuse me." And he's looking right at Adele Abrams. He says, "Could I ask you a question, please?" . . . Adele is shaking like a leaf. And she walks over to him.

EUGENE. Adele? He's talking to Adele Abrams?

KATE. And he says, "I wonder if your friend would care to dance with me?" . . . And she says, "You want *me* to ask her?" . . . And he says, "Please. I'm a little shy."

EUGENE. I don't believe it. I don't believe George Raft said that.

KATE. I swear to God. May I never live to see another day.

EUGENE. Even if it's true, it's out of the picture. An audience would never believe it.

KATE. Fine. So Adele says, "I'll ask her." . . . So she comes back and asks me . . . And I look at him and he smiles at me . . . And his eyes moved for the first time. Not fresh or anything, but he had the look of a man with a lot of confidence and I never saw that before. Scared the life out of me. So I walk over to him and he takes my hand and leads me out to the floor . . . Everyone in the

Primrose is watching. Even the band. Someone had to whisper, "Start playing," so they would begin . . . And they began. And we danced around that room. And I held my head high and my back straight as a board . . . And I looked down at the floor and up at the ceiling, but never in his eyes. I saw a professional do that once . . . His hands were so gentle. Hardly touching me at all, but I knew exactly when he wanted me to move and which way he wanted me to turn.

EUGENE. (*dropping the knitting and rushing to the radio*) Wait a minute! Wait a minute!

KATE. What are you doing?

EUGENE. I want you to show me how you danced. (*He turns on the radio and begins to search for appropriate music.*)

KATE. (*sitting down at the table*) Show you how I danced thirty-five years ago? I don't even *walk* like I did thirty-five years ago.

EUGENE. Come on. You dance every year with Pop at the Garment Industry Affair. Just show me how you danced with George Raft.

KATE. They danced differently in those days. They don't even do those steps anymore.

EUGENE. Not a whole dance. Two steps . . . One turn . . . (*He finds the right music. It is Benny Goodman's recording of "It Had To Be You."*) There! Listen! That's the perfect music . . . (*He crosses to KATE at the table.*) So he moved you gently around the floor.

KATE. Stop it, Eugene. I'm not in the mood.

EUGENE. (*holding out his arms to her*) Come on. I'll dance with you . . . I'm George Raft . . . (*He mimes slicking down his hair.*) Everybody is watching us . . . Don't let 'em down, Mom. (*KATE looks at EUGENE for a moment, listening to the music. Then she slowly stands and they begin to dance — awkwardly at first, then more gracefully.)*

KATE. You're holding me too tight . . . Don't push me . . . Just with your fingertips.

EUGENE. You're so graceful, Mom . . . I never knew you were so graceful. There's Adele Abrams. (*He waves.*) Adele? She's wonderful. (*They continue to dance.*)

KATE. Now turn me.

EUGENE. How?

KATE. Just let go. (*He lets go. She does a turn*) Now give me your hand. (*She is back in his arms for the finish of the number*) And then it was over. (*EUGENE turns off the radio. KATE is embarrassed, but flushed with excitement. He smiles at her*)

EUGENE. And then what did he say to you?

KATE. He said, "Thank you. It was my pleasure." And he walked away.

EUGENE. He didn't even ask for your name?

KATE. I didn't ask for his, why should he ask for mine? (*She sits at the dining table*) My God, I'm drenched in perspiration. In the middle of the winter. I don't know how I let you get me to do such things.

EUGENE. (*sitting on the sofa arm, opposite KATE*) Because you liked it. Why do you always stop doing the things that make you feel good?

KATE. What's the matter? Raising you and Stanley wasn't something that made me feel good?

EUGENE. There's other things besides raising a family, Ma.

KATE. Yeah. So I've heard . . . Alright. I want you in bed. And no more back talk. (*She collects the yarn and puts it away*)

EUGENE. You didn't finish the story. Did you get home before twelve?

KATE. No. The trolleys were running late. I came in almost twelve-thirty.

EUGENE. And what did your mom and pop say?

KATE. They didn't know. They decided to sleep over at her sister's house. Only Aunt Blanche came home. And she was fast asleep. I didn't tell anybody what I did . . . But in two days the news was all over the neighborhood. People were congratulating my mother. They treated her like her daughter was a movie star. She was angry with me, but she knew she couldn't say anything . . . But when I saw my grandmother, she winked at me, squeezed my hand and said, "I know, darling. I know." (*She turns off the dining room lights.*) So now do you believe I danced with George Raft?

EUGENE. Yeah. I believe you.

KATE. (*going up the stairs*) God, I'm exhausted . . . Never ask me that question again. Telling the story was harder than dancing with him.

EUGENE. (*following her up the stairs*) I think what you did that night was great . . . And you didn't get caught. So God didn't punish you. The movie has a happy ending.

KATE. (*standing at her bedroom door*) . . . The movie isn't over yet.

EUGENE. (*going into his bedroom and closing the door; to audience:*) I'll be honest about one thing. Dancing with my mother was very scary. I was doing what my father should have been doing with her but wasn't. And holding her like that and seeing her smile was too intimate for me to enjoy. Intimacy is a complex thing. You had to be careful who you shared it with . . . but without it, life was just breakfast, lunch, dinner and a good night's sleep. Most people would settle for that. Most people do . . . I was determined not to be most people.

(*He leaves his bedroom and goes into the bathroom. A lighting change shows us that the night has passed and the sun is coming up. It is early morning the next day. JACK, all dressed, comes out of his room. He tiptoes down the stairs, crosses to the back porch and brings out a large suitcase. He brings it into the living room. BEN, dressed, comes out of his room and down the steps. He stops when he sees JACK*)

BEN. Since when do you work on Sundays, Jack?

JACK. I didn't expect to see you up so early. I'm sorry, Ben. I haven't got time to talk.

BEN. (*coming into the living room*) Then take the time. Where are you going, Jack?

JACK. I'm leaving, Ben. I'm moving out.

BEN. I see . . . Did you explain this to Kate?

JACK. I thought I'd call her in a few days. I'd say all the wrong things now.

BEN. You mean in a few days you'll say all the right things? (*JACK goes to the closet for his coat.*) When did you pack your bag?

JACK. Friday night . . . when she was out shopping.

BEN. You should have told her, Jack. You could have saved money on food for the week.

JACK. (*coming back to his suitcase, coat on*) I've got to leave before she gets up.

BEN. So who tells her? Me? If you want me to tell her, you'd better pay me. And I get top money for telling my daughter her husband walked out on her.

JACK. This isn't just happening, Ben. This has been coming for a long time. She may be angry when I leave, but she won't be surprised.

BEN. You think she'll be angry? . . . You walk out on her after thirty-three years of marriage and you think all she'll be is *angry??* . . . If that's how much you understand her, then maybe she's better off without you.

JACK. What do you know about it? For thirty-three years you were a visitor in this house. You came, you ate dinner and you went home. You didn't live in that bedroom with us . . . No matter what anyone tells you, what happens to a man and wife happens in the privacy of that room . . . and not even God Himself is there all the time to listen.

BEN. You're making a mistake, Jack. No matter what she says, she'll never leave you . . . This thing with the other woman won't last . . . I know, because I've had enough other women in my life . . . Kate will find a way to deal with it. She'll ignore it, she'll pretend it's not happening. She'll live with you and not talk to you to protect her dignity, but she won't leave you . . . I'm her own father and I'm saying to you, *have* your affair until it's over, but don't break up what'll last you the rest of your life.

JACK. You don't understand. It's not an affair. I don't sleep with this woman. I did once, not now . . . She's sick. She'll live another five, six more months. Maybe not even that.

BEN. (*nods*) Maybe to you that's a noble gesture, but to me it stinks.

JACK. Don't be so God damn hypocritical. You've got a seventy-two-year-old wife living alone in Florida, and you stay here pretending you're martyring yourself for a political cause that you haven't been interested in for the last twenty years. I'm the last one to blame you . . . Where is it written that a man must love the same woman until the day he dies?

BEN. In the marriage vow he took.

JACK. If I took it, then you took it too, Ben.

BEN. True. And maybe I don't love anymore. Maybe I
am a hypocrite. I don't have another woman,
no . . . My mistress is my privacy. I am unfaithful with
a room upstairs that lets me do what I want. I'm having
an affair with peace and quiet . . . But you're right. I'm
no better than you.

JACK. (*at the front door with his suitcase*) I'm fifty-five
years old, Ben. I'm not ready for a room yet. I need to
run. I need to get away from myself and everything I was.
I have no more children to raise. I have nothing waiting
out there for me except one thing . . . Something else!
(*JACK starts to go out the front door.*)

BEN. I still think you're making a mistake, Jack. A big,
big mistake.

JACK. (*turning back*) Why?

BEN. . . . Because Kate is my daughter.

JACK. I'll call the boys tomorrow.

(*JACK goes. BEN sits on the sofa, then hears KATE
coming out of her bedroom. He hurries into the
kitchen. KATE comes out in a housedress, goes
downstairs and looks out the front door window for a
moment. BEN comes out of the kitchen with a roll on
a plate with butter on the side and a knife.*)

BEN. How long have you been up?

KATE. A few minutes. I heard Jack coming downstairs, I thought he must be hungry. Did you put up hot
water?

BEN. (*sitting at the table*) Certainly I put up hot water.
What am I, an invalid? (*He butters his roll.*)

KATE. You want some eggs?

BEN. No.

KATE. (*crossing to the back porch*) No eggs?

BEN. Why do you always ask me if I want eggs? If I wanted eggs, wouldn't I ask you?

KATE. It's too early in the morning, Poppa. Don't start in.

BEN. Listen, if it'll make you happy to make me eggs, make them. Scrambled, not too loose.

KATE. You just said you didn't want any.

BEN. I don't. I'm having them for you.

KATE. (*angrily*) Don't ask me to make you things if you don't want them. (*She catches herself.*) I'm sorry. I hardly slept last night.

BEN. I heard the music. I heard you dancing with Eugene. I forgot all about your grandmother giving you the dining room table.

KATE. You forget a lot of things. Poppa. You shouldn't have been listening.

BEN. I know. But I enjoyed it. I left my door open a crack . . . Some boys you got, Kate. You raised them good, believe me.

KATE. Where is Jack so long? Is he in the kitchen? No one lets me cook here anymore. (*She goes into the kitchen. BEN stares at his roll. KATE comes back to the table.*) Is he in the house?

BEN. No.

KATE. Where'd he go, for a walk?

BEN. No.

KATE. He's not in the house and he didn't go for a walk . . . So where'd he go on a Sunday morning? (*She looks at BEN, who hasn't moved. And suddenly she realizes . . . She turns away.*) Why did't you tell me? . . . You think I wasn't expecting it?

BEN. I didn't know how to say it . . . He's gone, Kate . . . He moved out . . . It's as simple as that.

(She stands there a moment, not saying a word. Then she goes out to the porch, lights a cigarette and looks out BEN goes into the kitchen. EUGENE comes out of the bathroom, fully dressed. His cold is gone. Time is in transition. He stands at the top of the stairs.)

EUGENE. *(to audience)* When Mom heard the news about Pop, she didn't cry, she didn't reach for anyone to hug, she didn't make a sound . . . When I was in the army, they told us, in battle, don't bother attending the wounded who were crying for help . . . Go to those who didn't make a sound. They were the ones in real trouble . . . *(KATE finishes her cigarette and goes into the kitchen. EUGENE comes down the stairs into the living room. To audience:)* . . . The winter moved on and so did our careers. As the temperature grew colder, Stan and I got hotter. They doubled our salary at C.B.S. and we were washing our hands in the same john as Arthur Godfrey . . .

(STAN comes running excitedly down the street and into the house. He sees EUGENE.)

STAN. Okay. Don't say a word. Just sit down.

EUGENE. What

STAN. Will you just sit down. Because you're not going to believe this. Go on. *(EUGENE sits.)* No. Stand up. This news is too important to be sitting.

EUGENE. *(getting up again)* What are you talking about?

STAN. Where's Mom? . . . *Mom!!* Come on inside. Grandpa? . . . Where's Grandpa?

EUGENE. He fell asleep on the kitchen table. *(KATE comes in from the kitchen and stands by the breakfront, looking at the two boys.)*

STAN. Mom! . . . Remember I once told you, you have to have faith in me . . . I knew talent when I see it and I knew right away that Eugene and I had it . . . I never gave up on us, did I? . . . Did I, Eugene?

EUGENE. No. Never . . . Except for the eight times you wanted to commit suicide.

STAN. (*hanging up his coat*) Except for those eight times, I was like a rock.

EUGENE. And once you smashed the typewriter with my baseball bat.

STAN. Except for the time I smashed the typewriter, I never lost heart, right?

EUGENE. Except for the time you lost heart.

STAN. But otherwise, I never faltered. Never gave up hope. So guess what I'm going to tell you?

EUGENE. You gave up hope.

STAN. We got "The Phil Silvers Show." You, me and two other writers . . . Two hundred dollars a week . . . Apiece . . . *APIECE!!* . . . That's four hundred dollars a week . . . Do you realize how much money that is?

EUGENE. *Three* hundred dollars a week?

STAN. (*hugging EUGENE*) Congratulate me, you lousy kid. I negotiated the whole deal myself. We don't even have to pay an agent.

EUGENE. You're incredible . . . When do we start?

STAN. Three weeks from Monday. They wanted to know if we thought we could double on "The Chubby Waters Show," but I turned them down. It's too much work.

EUGENE. We can handle it. Why don't we do it?

STAN. No! Big mistake. We spread ourselves too thin, we'll lose the quality. If we make good here, we'll get the big money later . . . So what do you think about this, Mom?

KATE. What do I think? . . . I got two geniuses, that's what I think.

STAN. (*kissing KATE*) Three geniuses, because you're the one who gave birth to us . . . That's why I think you should be living in New York, too.

KATE. New York? What are you talking about?

STAN. (*going to stand beside EUGENE*) Gene and I are moving next week . . . I signed the lease today. We'll be working night and day, it would be murder for us to come out *here* to visit you. The woman showed me a place two blocks away. Perfect for you and Grandpa. Before you say no, come and look at it.

KATE. In the first place, if your grandfather didn't go to Miami, he won't go to New York. In the second place, who do I know in the city?

EUGENE. Aunt Blanche.

KATE. Aunt Blanche lives on Park Avenue. I don't have clothes to visit Park Avenue . . . I have my friends here. I like the stores better. You know what they would charge me for chicken breasts in New York? Forget it.

STAN. I just want you to be happy, Mom.

KATE. You made me happy enough today. Too much happiness and I get scared.

STAN. (*slapping EUGENE's shoulder*) Come on upstairs. We've got things to talk about. (*EUGENE goes upstairs ahead of STAN.*)

KATE. What day are you moving?

STAN. Next Monday.

KATE. Did you call the movers?

STAN. (*on the stairs*) We're not taking any furniture, Mom. We're getting all new stuff. We're just taking our clothes.

KATE. You don't want the bureau? It's a beautiful

bureau. Your father and I bought that new in Bamberger's.

STAN. That was twenty-five years ago, Mom.

KATE. You don't want it, don't take it. I'll save it. Maybe your children will want it.

STAN. Gene's children. I'm not ready for marriage yet.

KATE. Well, get ready. If I don't get grandchildren, what did I need children for? (*KATE goes into the kitchen. STAN and EUGENE go into EUGENE's room.*)

STAN. (*closing the door*) I got other news, too. I saw Pop today. He was waiting for me outside C.B.S.

EUGENE. (*sitting on the bed*) No kidding. How is he?

STAN. The lady he was seeing? Audrey? They took her to the hospital yesterday. He said she won't last out the week.

EUGENE. That's too bad. How was Pop taking it?

STAN. He looked lousy. He asked about Mom. He asked if she was alright. Then he started to cry. We were in Louie's Restaurant on Madison Avenue. He grabbed my hand and held it. He sat there for half the lunch holding my hand. The waiter looked at us like we were a couple of lovers.

EUGENE. You think when this Audrey — you know — you think he'll come back to Mom?

STAN. No. I asked him. At least not for now. He said to me, "No, I can't go back to that house . . . Besides, she'd never take me back," he says.

EUGENE. Sure she would. She still loves him.

STAN. Maybe. But she's stubborn. Like Grandpa.

EUGENE. Why are they doing this to each other, Stan?

STAN. I don't know. Maybe he explains it all in the letters.

EUGENE. What letters?

STAN. He gave me two letters. One for me, one for you.

EUGENE. What's in it?

STAN. (*handing EUGENE a letter*) I don't know.

EUGENE. You didn't read yours?

STAN. He doesn't want us to. Not yet.

EUGENE. When can we read them?

STAN. After he dies.

EUGENE. After he dies?

STAN. He made me promise him that. I said, "If it's important, Pop, why can't you tell us what's in it now?" He said he just couldn't. We would have to wait.

EUGENE. Suppose he lives to be ninety? They'll turn yellow, we'll never be able to read it.

STAN. They're probably letters of apology. Explaining why he did what he did.

EUGENE. By then I'd be fifty-four. I wouldn't even care.

STAN. Or maybe the letters say he'll never forgive us for what *we* did. For my saying "Go to hell" to him.

EUGENE. He already forgave you. He held your hand in the restaurant . . . So? Are you going to wait until he dies to read it?

STAN. I'm going to try . . . What about you?

EUGENE. Suppose I die before him? Does he get his letter back?

STAN. You're funny, Gene. You've got a wonderfully inventive mind, but sometimes it lacks respect. (*STAN goes into his own room. He looks at his own letter, then puts it in his pocket, takes out a suitcase and packs. EUGENE turns his envelope over in his hands. Then he looks at the audience.*)

EUGENE. (*to audience*) It probably does. I was really confused. I always loved my father, but I didn't like him for leaving my mother and I was really sore at him for leaving me this thing . . . I sure didn't want him to die, but how else would I get to read the damn letter? I knew I was really angry when I thought about sending him a gift on Father's Day and printing on it, "Never Ever To Be Opened" . . . The following Monday was our last day in Brighton Beach. (*He puts on a jacket and puts the letter in the inside pocket. As he speaks, he takes out a suitcase from under the bed and packs. STAN comes out of his room with the suitcase and crosses downstairs. He gets their coats out of the closet.*) Stan and I didn't have much to take. We were going to throw out our old clothes, but Mom put them in a box in the basement. Just in case. Daughters of Socialists don't have too much faith in show business. (*EUGENE leaves his room and brings his suitcase downstairs. BEN comes out of the kitchen.*)

STAN. Where's Mom?

BEN. In the kitchen baking you two years' worth of cookies.

EUGENE. (*putting on his coat*) Remember your promise, Gramps. You're going to come to the studio to watch the first show.

BEN. Only if it's about something. If it's just funny, I'm not interested.

EUGENE. No, no. The first show is about a girl from Mount Holyoke. She meets a boy named Myron Trotsky.

STAN. (*sitting on the sofa arm*) Why did you tell him? Now he knows the ending.

BEN. You still like to kid me, you two. You think I never knew when you were kidding me? I'll tell you something. When you were kidding me, I was kidding you twice as much.

KATE. (*coming out of the kitchen carrying a large*

cardboard box tied with string) Don't jiggle the box too much. It makes crumbs.

EUGENE. (*Taking the box*) How much should we ask for them, Mom? We're going to sell them on the train.

STAN. No train. We're making *this* trip in a cab.

BEN. Don't let my friends see you getting into a cab.

STAN. Am I going to get a hug from you, Gramps?

BEN. A hug yet. You really want to humiliate me, don't you?

STAN. No. I just want to say goodbye. (*STAN hugs BEN and kisses his cheek, then steps away.*)

BEN. (*to EUGENE*) I suppose I'm going to get the same thing from you, heh?

EUGENE. Of course. I'm going to kiss you right on the lips. They're going to have to pull us apart. (*EUGENE hugs BEN and kisses his cheek, then steps away.*)

STAN. (*to KATE*) Hey! Broadway Momma! (*opens his arms*) Step right into these arms.

KATE. Yesterday he was a writer, today he's Clark Gable. (*STAN kisses KATE and gives her a long hug. Then he steps away.*)

EUGENE. I just want to say one thing, Ma . . .

KATE. Don't say anything. You know me. I don't deal with these things too good.

EUGENE. It's not that horrible. And it's quick . . . I love you. Okay? That wasn't so bad, was it? (*EUGENE kisses KATE and gives her a long hug.*)

STAN. Okay, come on, let's go! We're not moving to Budapest. We've got a party at four o'clock. (*EUGENE steps away from KATE and goes to his suitcase at the front door.*)

EUGENE. What party?

STAN. At C.B.S. Do you realize the gorgeous women we're going to meet today.

KATE. Stanley! He's got Josie. You leave him alone.

(*EUGENE opens the front door and sets his suitcase outside.*)

STAN. (*in the open door*) I was kidding, Mom. I won't let a single beautiful showgirl get near him. We'll call you in a few days . . . And, Grandpa, just so you know, I always knew when you were kidding me.

BEN. I knew when you knew. (*BEN and KATE exit into the kitchen. STAN brings his suitcase outside and stands beside EUGENE.*)

STAN. Come on. It's freezing.

EUGENE. I just want to look at the house for a minute.

STAN. I'm going to look for a cab. I don't care what it costs, this is one party I'm not missing . . . I told you we'd make it, didn't I? I picked Joe DiMaggio and us. Not bad, huh? (*He runs up the street to look for a cab.*)

EUGENE. (*to audience*) I knew then that no matter how many times I came back to see this house, it would never be my home again . . . Mom and Pop split up for good and never got back together . . . As a matter-of-fact, he remarried about two years later to a pretty nice woman. Mom would really be hurt if she heard me say that, but the truth is the truth . . . Grandpa found it rough going in his seventy-eighth year and finally surrendered to Capitalism and Miami Beach . . . He plays pinochle every day and donates half his winnings to the Socialist Party . . . Josie and I got married and we sleep each night with her hand lying gently across my chest. I won't even breathe for fear she'll move it away.

STAN. (*running down the street to EUGENE*) Gene! Come on! I got a cab!

EUGENE. I'm coming. I'm coming.

STAN. I never realized how cold it was out here before. (*STAN exits up the street, taking EUGENE's box of cookies with him.*)

EUGENE. (*to audience*) I didn't keep my promise to

Pop. I opened his letter and read it. He didn't apologize, and he wasn't mad at Stan and me for what we wrote. The only thing he wanted was for Stan and me to understand his side of the story . . . Only he never said what his side was . . . Contrary to popular belief, everything in life doesn't come to a clear-cut conclusion. Mom didn't do anything very exciting with the rest of her life except wax her grandmother's table and bask in the joy of her sons' success. But I never got the feeling that Mom felt she sacrificed herself for us. Whatever she gave, she found her own quiet pleasure in. I guess she was never comfortable with words like "I love you." A hard life can sometimes knock the sentiment out of you . . . But all in all, she considers herself a pretty lucky woman. After all, she did once dance with George Raft. (*EUGENE turns away from the house, grabs his suitcase and runs up the street to the cab.*)

Curtain

End of Play

COSTUME PLOT

EUGENE

Act I
Grey zippered jacket
Maroon/blue wool scarf
Grey knit gloves
Brown pants
Ecru/brown shirt
Maroon sweater
Brown lace-up shoes
Brown socks
Brown/orange/red print tie
Tan belt
Wristwatch

Act II-1
Rust/brown striped robe
Blue/cream flannel pajamas
White sweat socks
Brown slippers
Plaid hanky

Act II-2
Teal blue slacks w/ black belt
Green/pumpkin plaid shirt
Green pullover sweater
Repeat Act I shoes/socks/wristwatch

Act II-3
Add grey tweed jacket to above

STANLEY

Act I
2-Piece blue suit

103

Red print tie
Blue striped shirt
Lt./dk. blue socks
Brown slip-on shoes
Lt. grey overcoat
Dark grey fedora
wristwatch

Act II-1
Brown slacks
Brown/white striped shirt
Tan argyle socks
Tan/brown houndstooth jacket
Cocoa/yellow print tie
White pocket hanky
Mustard argyle sweater vest
Repeat overcoat & hat

Act II-2
Dark blue slacks
White shirt
Blue/red print tie
Blue-flecked jacket
Navy argyle socks

KATE

Act I
Blue/pink floral housedress
Blue/aqua full apron
Beige seamed stockings
Pink sweater w/ hanky
Brown shoes
Wristwatch & wedding ring

Act I-2
Pink rayon nightgown
Pink chenille robe
Lavender slippers

Act II-1
Navy/white dot dress
Navy heels
Navy cardigan sweater
Small blue stone earrings
Wristwatch
Grey overcoat
Grey knit gloves

Act II-2
Blue/green paisley housedress
Green cardigan sweater
Repeat navy shoes

Act II-3
Repeat housedress
Repeat Act I pink cardigan sweater
Yellow/green print full apron

JACK

Act I
Brown 3-piece suit
White shirt
Rust/green tie
Grey flannel coat
Grey wool scarf
Grey fedora
Black wing-tip shoes
Black leather gloves

Black shoe rubbers
brown socks

Act II-1
Grey 3-piece suit
Grey socks
Blue print tie
Repeat Act I shirt, shoes, coat, scarf, gloves, rubbers, hat

Act II-2
Repeat Act I suit and accessories
Green print tie

BEN

Act I
Grey slacks
Suspenders
Blue striped shirt
Blue print tie
Cocoa brown cardigan sweater
Grey socks
Brown house slippers
Taupe overcoat
Black galoshes
Grey fedora

Act I-2
Beige striped nightshirt
Repeat grey socks & slippers

Act II-1
Brown herringbone slacks
Brown/tan plaid shirt
Blue/pink print tie
Repeat cardigan, socks & slippers

Act II-2
Repeat above
Green/rust plaid shirt

BLANCHE

Act I
Red 2-piece suit
Cream sleeveless blouse
Black shoes
Brown suede galoshes w/ fur trim
Mink coat
Brown hat
Purse
Gloves
Hanky w/ lace trim

PROPERTY PLOT

Act I — Present

KITCHEN

1. Bowl of fruit with (1) real apple
2. 5 Dinner plates
3. Tray w/ pitcher of water 1/3 full; 5 water glasses
4. Tray of condiments
5. Plate of chicken broth w/ soup spoon
6. Bread plate w/ 6 slices of rye bread
7. Tray w/
   Plate #1 — pot roast sandwich, slice of pound cake
   Plate #2 — Pot roast sandwich, slice of pound cake, 12 glasses of seltzer water
8. Dinner plate w/ pot roast and vegetables
9. Small gift-wrapped gift
10. Tray w/ 2 teacups — saucer — 2 teaspoons, piece of pound cake, cake knife, creamer — $\frac{1}{2}$ full of milk
11. Teapot w/ hot tea — $\frac{1}{2}$ full
12. Wine glass $\frac{1}{2}$ full — red wine
13. Relish dish-3 whole pickles, 4 slices of pickle
14. Pitcher of fresh water and cups
15. Large box of cookies — under kitchen table
16. Jack's suitcase — in porch — upstage

DINING ROOM

SIDEBOARD

1. Folded freshly ironed tablecloth — right drawer
2. 5 Spoons, 5 forks, 5 knives — left drawer
3. 5 Napkins — left drawer

4. 2 Doilies — left drawer
5. Box of dates — second shelf — left
6. Sugar bowl w/ sugar — second shelf — right
7. 2 Candlesticks — under shelves — right
8. Dining room table — 5 chairs — pushed in
9. 6th Chair stage right of sideboard
10. Skein of wool in basket — lower left side of sideboard

LIVING ROOM

CLOSET

1. Ben's hat on shelf
2. Ben's coat — lapels facing stage left
3. Ben's galoshes — floor of closet
4. Kate's coat

SOFA

1. 2 Throw cushions — right end of sofa
2. Afghan over back of sofa — left end

UPSTAIRS

BEN'S ROOM

1. Brown paper bag w/ sheet
2. Pajamas
3. Pitcher of fresh water and glass
4. Box of Kleenex
5. Wastepaper basket

EUGENE'S ROOM

1. 3 Black lined pads — desk
2. 5 Pencils — desk
3. Exercise book — dresser

4. Bed — made up
5. Desk chair — under desk
6. Bathrobe — back of door
7. Suitcase — under bed

STANLEY'S ROOM

1. 4 Books and small pad — desk — downstage of typewriter
2. Typewriter — center on desk
3. Typing paper — upstage of typewriter
4. 3 Yellow pads — desk drawer
5. 6 Pencils — desk drawer
6. Small pencil sharpener — desk drawer
7. Suitcase — under bed

OFF RIGHT — Prop table

1. Manila envelope
2. 2 Sealed letters
3. Stanley's hat

COAT RACK

1. Eugene's coat and scarf
2. Stanley's coat
3. Jack's coat — scarf — gloves — rubbers

STAGE LEFT TABLE

1. Jar of honey
2. Mirror
3. Chair

Act II — Strike

INTERMISSION

STRIKE FROM KITCHEN

1. 5 Dinner plates
2. Tray of condiments
3. Plate of soup and spoon
4. Plate w/ 6 slices of bread
5. Plate w/ pot roast and vegetables
6. Tea tray—2 cups and saucers—teaspoons—cake—cake knife—creamer
7. Teapot
8. Glass of wine
9. Relish dish w/ pickles
10. Water glass—11 napkins—12 silverware

STRIKE FROM SIDEBOARD

1. Tray w/ water pitcher—4 glasses
2. Napkins
3. Tablecloth (to wardrobe for ironing)
4. Any silverware

STRIKE LIVING ROOM CLOSET

1. Ben's hat
2. Jack's coat—hat—scarf—gloves
3. Jack's rubbers

Act II—Preset

INTERMISSION

SET IN KITCHEN

1. Bowl of fruit
2. Bowl of nuts
3. Platter of sandwiches

4. Kaiser roll — butter — knife — on plate
5. Dish towel
6. Tray — tea service for five
7. Cup of hot tea — saucer — teaspoon — teabag (dry)
8. Bottle of polish
9. Polishing cloth
10. Cookie box

DINING ROOM

1. 5 Napkins — left drawer
2. 5 Spoons/forks — left drawer
3. 2 Doilies — right draws

CHECK

1. Candlesticks
2. Box of dates
3. Skein of wool in basket
4. Sugar bowl back on second shelf of sideboard

LIVING ROOM CLOSET

1. Kate's coat
2. Stanley's coat
3. Stanley's hat
4. Eugene's coat and scarf
5. Ben's galoshes

SOFA — CHECK

1. Throw cushions
2. Afghan throw

OFF RIGHT

1. Jack's coat — hat — gloves — rubbers

2. 2 Letters

OFF LEFT — CHECK

1. Jar of honey

INTERMISSION

STRIKE STANLEY'S ROOM

1. Tray of food
2. Manila envelope

STANLEY'S ROOM — CHECK

1. Suitcase — under bed
2. Jacket and tie — desk chair back
3. Shoe buffer

STRIKE — EUGENE'S ROOM

1. Sandwich on plate

RE-SET

1. 3 Pads to upstage end of desk
2. Pencils in holder
3. Make up bed
4. Exercise book on bed
5. Handkerchief on bed
6. Set chair at bed
7. Orange juice — on chair
8. Bottle of cold pills
9. Jacket on floor — upstage of bed

SECOND FLOOR

SCENE DESIGN
" BROADWAY BOUND"

114